THE TRIGGER

THE NINTH PETE CULNANE MYSTERY

S.L. Smith

SIGHTLINE PRESS

St. Paul, Minnesota

ISBN: 979-8-9868405-5-0

First Edition, September 2024

Printed in the United States of America

Cover designed by Christopher Smith

SIGHTLINE PRESS
St. Paul, Minnesota 55117
www.slsmithbooks.com

A special dedication to my cousin Maggie.
I valued our weekly conversations and
miss you always.

PROLOGUE

"This is why I became a cop," Pete said, tapping a front-page headline in the *St. Paul Pioneer Press* that said, "The Father Says the Police Are Wrong!" "Did you read this article, Katie?"

Pete was torn these days. In the final days of paternity leave after the birth of his son Teddy, his long-awaited firstborn, he missed his work as a homicide detective with the St. Paul Police Department. He missed the sense of fulfillment he experienced each time he and his partner, Martin Tierney, solved a case. He notably missed the opportunity to provide a measure of peace to the families suffering after a loved one was snatched from their lives without warning. Yet he dreaded returning to work, because of what it would do to the amount of time he could spend with Teddy.

Inevitably, the schedule he and Martin kept would rob him of the ability to track the day-to-day changes in his son, since at times he'd have to go for days without seeing Teddy while he was awake, playing with him, wrapping him in his arms, rocking him and singing him to sleep.

Yes, there was no doubt about it. He wanted to have his cake and eat it too.

He continued kicking around the idea of finding another job ... one with regular hours. After wrapping up one of the cases he and Martin worked on, the grateful owner of a large Twin Cities firm offered him a job as the head of security. The wages were a draw, but could he find the same level of satisfaction and fulfillment in that kind of work? He'd listed all the benefits as well as all the drawbacks. So far, all he'd accomplished was reminding himself why he valued his job and how hard it would be to leave it.

Could he be happy doing anything else? Could he abandon Martin? Could he be the father he was determined to be and remain a detective?

Katie interrupted his soul searching when she said, "Could there be merit to the claim of the father in that story? Were you ever wrong? Ever regret getting into police work? Pete, tell me why you became a police officer."

She knew Pete was struggling over the return to his work as a detective. She didn't want him to abandon police work and regret it later. But she didn't want him to remain a police officer if he'd feel trapped or discontented. She, of course, would go along with whatever he decided.

They continued living in the home where Pete had lived with his first wife, Andrea. She died when a drunk broadsided her car, taking her life and the life of their unborn baby.

After Pete proposed to Katie, they'd spent months looking for a new home, but finally agreed they liked this one better than anything they'd seen in their price range. As an alternative, they undertook a major update in the kitchen, including removing some hanging cupboards to create an open floor plan. They refaced the cupboards, changing them from dark brown to white, installed variegated light-gray marble countertops with streaks of white, and converted to stainless-steel appliances. Finally, they painted the walls a soft gray and changed the flooring to old gray hardwood. They completed the renovation by replacing Pete's dining room table with Katie's ebony, countertop-height table with black-leather-padded chairs.

While Katie never felt uncomfortable in what had been Pete and Andrea's home, those changes made the home feel like hers.

After pouring Pete a large mug of coffee and fixing a mug of herbal tea for herself, she settled in across the table from him. She didn't want to miss a word. "I've heard bits and pieces, but I want to hear the whole story," she said. It occurred to her that she should record this for Teddy, but figured there would be plenty of opportunities for that.

"Go back to the very beginning, Pete. Okay?"

"Are you sure you don't want to put on your jammies and climb into bed before I begin? I know these days you're sleep deprived."

"No more than you. Go ahead."

That said, Katie pulled her chair in close to the table. That was something she hadn't been able to do for months. Then she leaned forward, and clasped her hands. She was determined to catch every nuance in a story that, despite their time together, remained a mystery to her.

Pete settled back on his chair, smiled, and began, "Once upon a time, in a land far, far away ..."

ONE

Setting the Stage

Pete winked at Katie, "I was enthralled with baseball for as far back as I can remember. I followed the Minnesota Twins and never missed a game—preferably on TV, otherwise on the radio. If I couldn't do either, I may have thrown a temper tantrum. You'd have to ask Mom."

Katie laughed and said, "If you did, the only person less likely to admit that is Grandma Jackie."

Pete chuckled and said, "Grandma Jackie gave me a compact portable radio when I was five. With that radio, I biked around the neighborhood, rode my skateboard, you name it—while listening to the Twins. Dad and Grandpa Culnane often took me to the Metrodome stadium to see the Twins. Grandpa always got me a program and taught me how to use the scorecard. I don't know how but, by some miracle, Dad got hold of two tickets for the sixth game of the 1987 World Series. Being able to attend that game with him blew me away with excitement. The Twins fell behind, but they won that game and the series. That game held some of my favorite memories—being there with Dad and watching our team on their way to winning the World Series for

4

the first time. Kent Hrbek, Dave Winfield, Jack Morris, and Paul Molitor were all high on my list of favorite Twins players. That those Minnesota boys made it into the major leagues encouraged me to think I could too.

"I also loved *playing* baseball. My radio, a baseball and my glove were my most-prized possessions. Dad had begun playing catch with me when I was barely more than a toddler. He was soon giving me pointers on throwing and fielding. When I was ten, he started taking me to batting cages to practice my swing. With Mom playing first base with us, Dad taught me how to execute a double-play turn. We spent hours working on that turn. I'll never forget how proud I felt in high school when my coach told me he'd never seen a 'sweeter turn.'

"Dad and Mom both supported my aspiration to play in the major leagues. They came to all my games in grade school, Little League, and high school. They even brought Grandpa and Grandma Culnane and Grandma Jackie to a few of my faraway college games. Grandma Jackie was a huge supporter. Mom told me that the ladies who played bridge with her were threatening to find a replacement for her, because she called in a sub so often during baseball season so she could see me play."

Pete shook his head and laughed.

"She always had her priorities!" Katie chuckled.

"I could pick out Grandpa's gravelly voice amidst the cheers. I was so lucky to have such a strong support group."

Katie said, "Please tell me more about your Culnane grandparents. I know far more about Grandma Jackie."

Pete smiled. He felt touched that Katie wanted to hear more about his family and his past, so he did as she requested.

"Well, Grandma Jackie's husband, Grandpa Jack, died more than a decade before I was born. So Grandpa Culnane is the only grandpa I ever knew. We always had a special relationship and spent a lot of time together when I was young. He pitched to me, and we played catch for hours.

"One afternoon when I was about eight, Grandma, Grandpa, and I went swimming at Lake Nokomis and then headed for the Dairy Queen on Cedar. At an intersection, while waiting for the light to change, a woman pushing a baby buggy along with her little girl, who was about four, came up alongside us. Suddenly, the little girl saw a friend, and she ran into the street, oblivious to the traffic."

Katie winced.

"Grandpa must have had an eye on her because he quickly stepped down off the curb, scooped her up with a sweep of his right arm, and was back alongside me in a split second. As you know, Grandpa's a big guy, but that day he was as graceful as a ballet dancer as he rescued that little girl. She started crying, while her mother threw her arms around Grandpa and thanked him. Grandpa told her he was glad the child was safe. Then he crouched down face-to-face with the little girl and said, 'I grabbed you, because I saw you could have been badly hurt, Sweetheart. These cars are so much bigger than you and me. They can't stop as fast as we can. I'd hate to see you get hurt and not be able to play with your friends for a very long time.' He looked her in the eyes and added, 'Promise that from now on you'll wait for a green light.' She nodded and ran to her mom."

Pete paused and said, "Grandpa was so great at explaining things to little kids."

Then he said, "Here's a good example that illustrates the kind of relationship we had. At a Little League game he attended, I struck out twice in a row. I was furious about not being able to hit anything that pitcher threw, and I threw the bat in frustration.

"After the game, Grandpa waited until we were alone to tell me that he was ashamed of me when I threw that bat. I sputtered, 'But Grandpa ...' He kept talking, telling me that such behavior was poor sportsmanship, and that's never acceptable. 'What if your bat hit and injured someone?' he asked, looking hard at me. I told him I knew it wouldn't, because 'I had control over it.'

"'So you had control over the bat, but not over yourself?' he asked. Then he added in a serious tone, 'I hope I never see another display of poor sportsmanship out of you. Understand?' I nodded of course, and he said, 'Not to dwell on the negative, but what if the bat had slipped as you were throwing it? What if it hit someone and caused a serious injury? That can happen, you know.' I nodded again, but he wasn't done. 'Had you injured someone, how would you feel? Could you forgive yourself? Did throwing the bat make you feel better?'

"I told him, 'No, you're right, Grandpa. I'll never do it again. Sorry I disappointed you.' He flashed a warm smile and said, 'It's rare, Pete, but now that we've talked about it, how about if we let it go?' I smiled, and he gave me a high five. I will always treasure that conversation."

Smiling, Katie said, "What a sweet moment between the two of you."

Pete nodded, remembering, then he continued, "Grandpa got up at six o'clock every morning. You could have set your watch by it. I was usually up about that same time when I stayed overnight with them.

7

Grandma was more of a night owl and slept until about nine. I remember one morning, Grandpa and I were in the kitchen and he was making coffee when he looked out the window and saw smoke coming from the roof of a neighbor's house. He told me to call 911 and report a fire in Mary Rothsay's home, and he rattled off the address. As he ran out the door, he told me to stay inside and tell Grandma to stay there with me ... where it was safe. He, of course, knew I wanted to follow him."

Katie nodded and said, "Of course."

"I made the call and kept watch at the window. Grandpa found Mary's back door locked, so he climbed through a side window. I saw flames shooting out of Mary's roof, and I was scared for Grandpa and Mary, but then Grandpa came bursting out the back door, carrying Mary. Just then, Grandma ran into the kitchen, having heard the sirens, and I pointed to Mary's house. Grandma looked and started for the back door. I said quickly that Grandpa wanted us to wait in here, that he already rescued Mary. Grandma still looked alarmed when she said, 'Of course he did.'

"Grandpa saved Mary's life. She'd been overtaken by smoke inhalation. That was my first understanding of the critical emergency work done by first responders."

Katie smiled and asked, "Did that inspire you to become a hero like your grandpa?"

Pete said, "I'm not a hero, and Grandpa wasn't the only hero in my family. Grandpa's brother, my great uncle Pete, was a hero to me too. I don't think I've told you much about Grandpa's big brother."

Katie shook her head and asked, "Are you named after him?"

Pete nodded. "*Uh huh*, and grateful for the honor. We called him, 'Pete the candy man.' He was a distributor for the Curtis Candy Company, and every time we saw him, he had a pocketful of candy samples for us. He was a regular attendee at my Little League and grade school baseball games, and also a big Twins fan. He took me to the Metrodome at least two or three times a month. He helped feed and heighten my desire to play in the major leagues. His favorite seats were close to the Twins' dugout and so close to the players. I waved at my favorite players as they returned to the dugout. Sometimes one waved back, and Uncle Pete smiled and poked me in the ribs. He told me to remember how good that feels when I reach the majors. When there was publicity about the Orioles playing the next year at Camden Yards, he wondered when the wrecking ball would attack Wrigley Field. He decided the two of us had to make a trip to Chicago to see the Cubs play there before it was too late. He told me to save my nickels, because I'd be responsible for buying the peanuts."

Pete's smile vanished and he sighed. "We never made that trip. One night, in the early morning hours, I heard the phone ring. I jumped out of bed and ran to the kitchen to grab it, wondering why Mom or Dad hadn't answered the one in their room. It was Aunt Lydia. She asked for Dad, and I knew from her voice that it was bad news. I ran to wake Dad and tell him Aunt Lydia was on the phone. He was out of bed like a shot. I don't know what Aunt Lydia said, but Dad told her to call 911. He grabbed clothes and his billfold. Dressing as he ran for the garage, he told Mom to call Uncle Pete's pastor and his doctor, request they go to the St. Joe's Hospital ER, and say he'd meet them there. I went back to my room and started crying and praying. Not sure which I did harder. I was so afraid I was going to lose Uncle Pete."

Katie's eyes misted, seeing the pain in Pete's face as he recalled that night.

"I didn't fall back to sleep. I just cried and begged God to let me see Uncle Pete again. Mom took one look at me in the morning and wrapped her arms around me. 'They took him into surgery,' she said as she hugged me, 'and they're doing everything possible. Right now, they're optimistic.'

"I spent the day at home waiting for any news about Uncle Pete. Tried reading a book and listening to a Twins game. Neither succeeded in taking my mind off Uncle Pete. When the phone finally rang, I cringed in fear and went looking for Mom. I found her sitting at the dining room table. One look at her face told me the news wasn't good. I sat quietly across from her and waited. She finally looked up and said that they couldn't save Uncle Pete. He had an abdominal aneurysm that burst. He came through the surgery just fine, but afterwards they couldn't revive him. I cried so hard I couldn't catch my breath.

"Mom put an arm around my shoulders and said, 'I know you loved him, Pete. We all did, and you know he thought the world of you. He told so many stories about the time he spent with you and how proud he was of the good and kind person you're becoming.'

"I don't remember if that made me feel better or worse. When Dad got home, I could tell he'd been crying. I'd never actually seen him cry before. He took one look at me, pulled me close, and held me that way for several minutes. Then he said, 'We can do this, buddy. You help me, and I'll help you. Is it a deal?' I couldn't speak, but I nodded.

"A few weeks later, he said he knew something was bothering me and asked if I wanted to talk.

"I admitted hating myself for missing my last chance to see Uncle Pete, due to a baseball practice. He hugged me and said, 'None of us expected we'd lose Uncle Pete so soon. He would be so sorry that you are feeling guilty about this. He sure loved watching you play. You still want to play big league baseball someday, right?'

"I sniffed and agreed, and he said that Uncle Pete would never want to interfere with my baseball aspirations.

"Dad hugged me and said, 'Next time, don't keep it locked up inside for so long.'

"From then on, I thought of Uncle Pete watching in the wings as I played baseball, and I kept my dream alive. I had decided early on that I wanted to go to Notre Dame. I wanted to play second base where there's usually lots of action. But I'd have played any position— even a quiet spot like right field.

"I felt ecstatic when Notre Dame offered me an athletic scholarship. But then reality slapped me in the face. The remaining cost per year, between tuition, room, and board, was mind-boggling. Mom, Dad, and I had a long talk. They said that with the money they'd set aside, student loans, and by cutting some corners at home, we'd manage. It was tempting, but I decided it wasn't fair to them. I was afraid they'd need to take out a mortgage on the home they'd been so happy to finally own free and clear."

Katie grinned and said, "That sounds like the practical and selfless guy I know."

Pete chuckled. "The fact I'd always been a saver also played a role in that decision. I didn't want to graduate with tens of thousands of dollars in college debt, even if a major league contract might permit me to pay it off quickly. What if I didn't make it into the majors? A few days later, an acceptance letter arrived from St. Jerome's University, offering a more generous baseball scholarship. With my savings and the college fund Mom and Dad set aside for me, I could swing that without taking out college loans ... as long as I was willing to forgo having a car and a few other niceties. At the time, I could not have imagined that selecting a small Catholic college in rural Minnesota would end up putting my life in danger and radically altering my chosen career."

"Danger?" Katie asked quickly, "What do you mean by your life was in danger?"

"Hang on. We're getting there." Pete smiled.

Two
Introductions

"**F**ast forward to the spring semester of my freshman year. I played third base, rather than my preferred second, but I was thrilled at having made the varsity team. The guy playing second was a senior. I played the position better than that guy, but he hit more long balls. I told myself I could move to second once he graduated. I still aspired to being drafted into the majors.

"But thanks to Dad, I also started college with a backup plan. He helped me realize that, even though I was a very good second baseman, the major leagues only have room for a few of them. I always liked the sciences and math, so I decided my backup plan would be to do something in one of those areas—maybe architecture. But I still hoped I'd play baseball ... or at least be a coach in the major leagues. I was working my way through all that when something happened that changed my mind and established the path I'd follow ... at least to this point.

"Athletes often hung around together not only at practices, while training and during games, but other times as well. We ate together, some of us studied together, and we spent most of our time with others playing our sport when we weren't in class or sleeping. During the spring semester of my freshman year, I had classes when all my buddies ate lunch. I wasn't thrilled about that, but I wasn't willing to mess up my class schedule to get around it. Too much trouble, and a cost-benefit analysis couldn't have justified it. Besides, it would only last a semester.

"It actually turned out to be a blessing in many ways. The first day of the new semester, I hurried into the Commons. Everything was served a la carte there, as opposed to The Refectory, where it was a flat eight dollars a meal. I was into economizing even back then.

"I looked around to see if I knew anyone. I didn't. The place was pretty empty, but I saw some tables with two or three guys. Way off in a corner all by himself was a guy who seemed to be concentrating intently on his tray. Figuring I had nothing to lose, I headed over and asked if he'd mind if I sat with him.

"His eyebrows shot up. He looked taken aback, amazed and he asked, 'Here, with me?'

"When I nodded, he said, 'Sure, why not?'

"I introduced myself, and he said, 'Yeah, I know who you are. You play third base. I never miss a home game, and I go to some of the practices. I haven't seen you commit a single error.'

"He said he'd had his heart set on being a major leaguer and spent a couple years in Little League— warming the bench. When he discovered that he liked and had an aptitude for computers, he said that was his 'saving grace.'

"I told him I was jealous, because I knew only enough about computers to get along—and that was barely. You should have seen the way his face lit up. He told me his name was Sterling Callaway, and everyone called him Bud. Turned out Sterling is his mom's family name, and she thought naming him Sterling would be a great way to honor her family. Bud chuckled and said he could have thought of at least a hundred better ways to do that, rather than saddling a kid with a name like Sterling. He was thankful she hadn't named him after her mother's family. Then his name would be Zumbrota. He said he'd have been ten before he learned how to spell it and laughed again.

"He said I should let him know if I ever needed help with computer stuff. Then frowning, he said that learning about computers had actually turned into 'a life-or-death struggle' for him. I asked what he meant, and he explained how it happened. I sat there with my mouth hanging open as he told me.

"When we got up to go, I asked if he'd be there at the same time the next day. His answer was 'Yes,' so we planned to eat together again."

Katie said, "Don't leave me hanging. Tell me about Bud's 'life-or-death' struggle."

Pete winked and said, "I was waiting for you to ask."

"Bud's dad sold real estate and had a take-home computer provided by his employer. This was back when home computers were an oddity. Bud was enthralled by the device. His bedroom and his dad's home office were both in the basement, and one night the temptation was just too great. After everyone else was in bed, Bud was experimenting with his dad's computer and somehow reformatted the hard drive. He knew his dad would be furious—at best. In an effort to save his hide, he spent the entire night determining how to undo what he'd done. In the process, he learned a ton about computers, and found it so satisfying that he continued expanding his expertise. Bud, of course, didn't say it that way, but that's the bottom line."

Katie said, "Imagine how scared he was while scrambling to undo what he'd done by mistake."

Pete agreed, "I couldn't have figured it out, despite the impending repercussions. That lunch was the start of our friendship. Our schedules matched four days each week, so we ate lunch together on those days. We ate the same stuff, hamburgers and fries, hot dogs and chips, pizza, stuff like that, and we almost always drank Coke. Bud was usually pretty quiet, but gradually opened up, and I really enjoyed getting to know him. We talked about St. Jerry's, our hometowns, our families, you name it. He grew up in Madison, Wisconsin. He told me about swimming in Lake Michigan, snowmobiling out in the country and along trails, and cross-country skiing. His dad was into restoring old cars, and he helped. I learned a lot from him as our friendship grew. He even invited me to spend spring break with his family, but my baseball schedule made that impossible.

"One day I asked him to hang around after my next home game, and I'd introduce him to the other players. He said, 'You'd do that?' and I said, 'You bet.' He was really happy.

"I was a little worried that some of the guys might give Bud a hard time, so I decided to set the stage. I talked about his phenomenal computer expertise and how much he helped me. I said I thought he might even consider helping some of them ... Well, almost everyone has computer issues from time to time. The guys all welcomed Bud like a long-lost brother. He became a second team mascot. I'll never forget how much he liked hanging with me and the other players.

"In addition to computers, he was amazingly detail- and numbers-oriented, and he began using those skills to help the pitchers and hitters on the team. I realized this after the batting average of one of the best hitters on the team took a nosedive.

"Bud took Randy aside and told him that, with few exceptions, when the count was three and two (that is three balls and two strikes), he swung at the next pitch. Randy did that because he believed with a three-two count, the pitcher was hard-pressed to put the next pitch in the strike zone. That might have been true, if it hadn't been for the fact many opposing teams seemed to be privy to Randy's willingness to swing at the next pitch if it was anywhere near the plate. They used it against him by, according to Bud, pitching him high and inside on the next pitch—and Randy couldn't hit those pitches which he'd otherwise have ignored. It took quite the sales job for Bud to convince Randy, but ultimately Randy's batting average took off.

"Austin was one of the pitchers Bud advised, after seeing the way he held the ball, reared back, and his delivery telegraphed the pitch he was throwing. Bud spent hours helping Austin understand his analysis and conclusions, and he eventually did better as well.

"After Bud provided similar pointers to several other players, the coaches heard about him and his tips, and he became the team's statistician.

"Another teammate, Chad, was struggling with calculus, and Bud started tutoring him. At the time, Bud was studying differential equations. Don't even ask me what that's about. I'm nowhere near that league." Pete rolled his eyes. "Anyway, Bud and Chad became good friends.

"St. Elizabeth's, our sister school, was a little more than a mile away. Our tuition included any classes we took there, and their students could take classes at St. Jerome's. A snub-nosed bus called The Link ran back and forth between the campuses. Students from both schools frequented the same off-campus locations. The most popular was Stuart's Pub and Grill, because they freely served underage kids, and it was a good place for guys to meet girls and vice versa. Lots of us on athletic scholarships hung out there, but we stuck with pop—for fear of losing our scholarships. Bud was on an academic scholarship, and he was cautious too. Some, however, were fearless. I wasn't one of them."

Katie nodded knowingly.

"I think Bud's first-ever date happened when I introduced him to the friend of a friend at Stuart's. They hit it off instantly and soon began meeting there regularly. I'll get back to her later.

"Meanwhile, my computer started locking up, and nothing I tried seemed to work. I was under pressure, due to the deadline for a paper. I mentioned it when I ate lunch with Bud one day. He said, 'No sweat' and promised to fix it after practice.

"For as long as I'd known him, whether or not he attended our practices, Bud always hiked through the woods after classes before settling down to study. He said it helped him relax and clear his head. Half expecting to see him at practice, I was disappointed when he didn't show. But I figured, if he didn't come to my room before dinner, I'd pick him up and we could eat together."

Pete blew out a long, slow breath. "I didn't see him before dinner, and we didn't eat together. In fact, the last time I saw Bud was at lunch that Wednesday."

THREE
Shocking News

Pete shook his head and, seeing he looked stricken, Katie leaned in close.

"After wrapping up an assignment I could do before Bud fixed my computer, and wondering why I hadn't heard from him, I left to find him. As I closed my door, I noticed a bunch of somber-looking guys at the end of the hallway. I figured someone flunked a test or was dumped by a girlfriend, and they were commiserating. When one of them signaled to me to join them, I waved him off; I was on a mission to find out why Bud hadn't shown. This wasn't like him, so there had to be an explanation. Was he tutoring Chad? Had it taken longer than expected?

"I sprinted to his dorm, feeling far more nervous than I should have over a malfunctioning computer. He lived in Anderson Hall, and I was in Aquinas. There was less than a city block between the two dorms, but I was winded by the time I reached his. I think I held my breath the whole way.

"Rounding the corner to his room, I saw two police officers standing outside his door, and I rushed over to make sure Bud was fine.

"The officers spoke in hushed tones as I approached, and I heard several muffled voices coming from inside Bud's room.

"I asked the officers, 'What's the deal?' while reaching to knock on Bud's door.

"An officer the size of a tank grabbed my jacket, pulled me away from the door, and asked what I thought I was doing.

"I told him I had to talk to Bud. His door was slightly ajar, and I tried to see into his room. But the officer spun me around and said, 'Mighty nosy, aren't you?'

"I told him Bud didn't show for a meeting, and I was there to get him.

"He said, 'Sorry, Bud isn't going anywhere.'

"Right away, I thought that meant that Bud was in trouble and they were arresting him, so I quickly told the officer I was positive that Bud hadn't done anything illegal.

"He asked how long I'd known Bud and how I knew what he would and wouldn't do.

"Since I felt confident that in the three months since I met Bud, I'd gotten to know him as well as anyone at St. Jerome's, I told the officer that we were good friends, that Bud loved school and computers, that he had big plans for finding a job that would make use of his computer expertise. I said he was looking forward to spending summer break doing an internship at Microsoft and was thrilled and proud to have accomplished a coup like that. I explained that he'd never do anything to screw it up, then I asked impatiently, '*Now* can I see him?'

"The officer put a hand on my shoulder and said, 'Sorry, son, he's dead.'

"I felt like someone just punched me in the gut, and my legs turned to rubber. I collapsed against the wall, trying to stay on my feet. Choking back tears, I asked, 'What happened?'

"He said they didn't know yet, that they were investigating Sterling's death. 'It would help if you answered my questions. I assume you want to know what happened, don't you?'

"Overwhelmed by the news about Bud, I yelled, 'Of course I do!' I felt like someone had dropped a ton of bricks on my head. I'd never dealt with the death of someone my age.

"The officer asked if Bud had been depressed and if so for how long.

"'No way!' I said. 'I just told you about his internship. He was flying high.'

"'I understand he lost a grandfather and wasn't dealing with it very well,' he said. 'Some of us take the loss of a loved one really hard.'

"I asked him, 'Why are you asking these questions?' I wanted to know where this was headed, but if what I suspected was true, I dreaded the answer. He stood looking at me, but he didn't respond. Perhaps he didn't like me questioning him.

"I took a long breath, then asked, 'You're not suggesting he killed himself, are you? He'd never do that!' I told him that when Bud's paternal grandpa died near the end of last summer, Bud took it hard, but we'd talked about it, and he was doing much better. And he was *never* suicidal.'

"The officer responded, 'Like I said, some guys can't cope with a loss like that.' Then he asked, 'What else was bothering him? I heard he was having trouble with some of his classes.'

21

"'You're kidding, right? Who told you that?' I felt totally mystified. I said there was no way he was having trouble with any of his classes. I told him that Bud used to laugh about failing a test if he got an A-minus. I insisted, 'The guy's a genius from math to physics, from political science to philosophy.'

"'Perhaps he talked a good game,' the officer suggested. 'Perhaps he'd been having trouble lately ... maybe the death of his grandfather made it harder for him to study, or concentrate, or hold onto information.'

"I told him Bud had a photographic memory, and I was positive he would have told me if he was having those sorts of problems ... that we talked about everything ... that I knew him better than anyone, except his family ...that he told me whenever he had a spat with his brother or sister, what his parents fought about, and why he had so much trouble forgiving himself when his grandpa died so unexpectedly ... really personal stuff like that.

"The officer asked, 'Why did he have trouble forgiving himself when his grandpa died?'

"I explained that Bud told me in private, and I wouldn't ... I couldn't share that. 'All I'll say,' I told him, 'is that we talked about it, and Bud had definitely moved on.'

"But the officer kept attacking that question from a thousand angles. I refused to provide any more details. He asked all about Bud's brother, sister, and parents. I said I hadn't met any of them, but I knew Bud and his brother were close and spoke a lot. I said his older sister got married right after she graduated from Northwestern, and she worked at some bank in Madison or Milwaukee. I said I knew Bud was close to his parents, and they 'expected great things from him.' Bud told me that.

"Reacting to that, the officer quickly asked if Bud was under pressure and stressed as a result of his parents' expectations, and I said that no one expected more from Bud than Bud himself.

"He came back with, 'So, he was under a lot of *self-induced pressure.*'

"I was getting so frustrated with the questions. I said I didn't think Bud was under any more pressure than the rest of us. 'In fact,' I'd insisted, 'because learning came so easy for him, I think he was under less than most of us. Why all these questions?' I demanded.

"He ignored my question and asked if Bud often hiked the trails along the river bluffs. I said Bud did that every day after his last class, that it was his way of relaxing and collecting his thoughts.

"Then he wanted to know if I usually went with him and I said, 'Wouldn't that defeat the purpose for those walks?'

Katie's eyebrows showed her reaction to Pete's speaking that way to a police officer.

"That made the officer a bit testy, but it didn't stop him. He asked if I'd ever gone on one of Bud's hikes. I said I'd never gone on his after-classes hikes, but I had walked with him along the bluffs. And his questions kept coming. He asked if Bud was a risk taker ... if he liked to screw around and take chances while walking along the bluffs. I said I'd never seen him do that. Then he asked why Bud would choose that location 'when there are plenty of safe places to walk?'

"By then I figured I knew *where* whatever happened to Bud had happened. And I knew that he didn't commit suicide. I answered the officer, saying that it was a secluded, safe place, as long as you didn't get reckless, and the seclusion was beneficial.

"He asked how many times I'd walked there with Bud, and I said maybe a half dozen. I explained the trail was at least ten or fifteen feet from the cliffs, so it was perfectly safe.

"He then asked me what 'Sterling' liked to talk about, and I told him that Bud had it all put together. He knew exactly where he was going and how to get there. Thankfully the officer left it at that. He didn't delve into any on-and off friendships Bud had with some of my teammates. Those were the guys who appreciated Bud when they were on a hitting streak or when their earned run average was on its way down. The same players were at times angry when either was headed in the wrong direction. I avoided the subject, confident neither was sufficient grounds for murder.

"Next the policeman asked more about Bud's parents. By then, I just needed to get away. I needed to wrap my mind around the fact that I'd never see Bud again, never have another heart-to-heart with him. I was glad my best answer was that they should talk to his brother, Winston. After all, he knew far more about his family than I ever could.

"The officer insisted another perspective (mine) was always helpful. So I had to spend five or ten minutes more sharing what I knew about Bud's family. It wasn't much, only his one brother Winston was two years older than him, and his sister Eleanor was six years older. We'd commiserated about having big sisters who thought they were our second mothers and ordered us around. I told the officer I envied Bud for having a brother. I always wanted one. Win and Bud were radically different. Bud was into computers, and Win was into girls and resurrecting junk cars. Bud was so shy, he went to great lengths to avoid interacting with girls—and dating. He looked up to Win, who he said often provided 'fatherly' advice.

"Based on what Bud told me, his parents were very close, did everything together, and rarely argued. When they did, it was usually about him. His mom believed they should give him every opportunity to capitalize on his computer expertise. His dad argued that Bud first needed to 'find out what the real world was all about.' Bud said that was a direct quote. He believed his dad's 'real world' was not the world in which we currently live. Just the same, based on the way he talked about them, he loved and respected his dad, mom, brother, and sister."

Looking at Katie tenderly, Pete added, "Since Win and Bud were so close, I wondered why Win hadn't helped Bud through his grandfather's death. I planned to ask one day but never had the chance."

He sighed and paused long enough to take a drink of the coffee he'd ignored and said, "Glad I like it lukewarm."

Then he smiled, reached across the table, squeezed Katie's hand, and asked, "Had enough, yet?"

"Not even close, and I have a question. Why did Bud have trouble forgiving himself after his grandpa died?"

FOUR
A Chance to Help Bud

After stretching, then crossing his arms on the table, Pete said, "I don't think Bud would mind, so here goes. Bud and his family were close with his grandparents on both sides. Of course, I could identify with that. One Sunday, his family went to visit his paternal grandparents, but Bud stayed home. He was scrambling, trying to wrap up a piece of software he was designing, and couldn't bear to set it aside. He was so close to completing it. Well, as it turned out, that would have been his last opportunity to see that grandpa, because he died four days later. Bud was angry with himself for placing a 'stupid software program' ahead of his grandpa.

"We talked about that a lot in the early days of our friendship. I told him it was reasonable to be angry with himself if his grandpa had been ill or if there was any other reason to think it might be the last time he'd see him. I said if he was to blame, perhaps his dad was even more at fault for not insisting that he go that day.

"Bud said his dad knew he'd spent every available minute on that project. He'd understood. So I asked him if his grandpa would have understood that too, and he

26

said, 'Hell yes!' His grandpa was very impressed with the things he could do with a computer. He'd even spent one whole afternoon at Bud's house, asking question after question, getting a feel for what Bud could accomplish with a computer. Bud said, 'Honestly, it blew him away.'

"I said, 'So what you're saying is your dad and your grandpa understood, but you can't?'

"Bud responded, 'You just don't get it.'

"I countered with, 'Perhaps you're the one who doesn't get it. Although you'd have liked to see your grandpa, you were in the middle of something important to you, and you figured there would be plenty of other opportunities, correct?'

"Bud said, 'Yeah,' and looked teary, and I persisted, 'In that case, what you're guilty of is not being able to foresee the future. Maybe you're guilty of not being God. Or maybe you should be angry with God for not sending you an email, ensuring you didn't make that mistake. Shame on you, God!' I said, exaggerating my facial expression and looking heavenward.

"Pete laughed as he explained, "Bud punched my right arm so hard, I wasn't sure I'd be able to throw a baseball with anything on it the next day. He must have thrown every ounce of his body weight into it. I honestly couldn't imagine how he delivered a punch like that. I was glad he'd targeted my arm, not my nose or one of my eyes. Then Bud smiled and said, 'Maybe you're right,' and he sighed.

"That was the last time he brought up the subject, but I didn't let it go. A week or two later, I asked if he was still struggling with his grandpa's death. He smiled and said 'God responded to my email. He told me to stop torturing myself before I eliminated *all* the time

He'd so carefully planned for me to suffer in Purgatory.'
Bud grinned and thanked me for helping him work
through it.

"I'll never forget that smile. I was happy to have
done something to make his life better. His friendship
added so much meaning and enjoyment to mine."

FIVE
Back to the Story

"**O**kay," Pete said, "returning to where I left off in Bud's dorm with the police. At that point, I must have looked either exhausted or pretty shaken. The police officer gave me his card, told me to call if I remembered or heard anything else about Bud that might explain his death, and he let me go. By the time I reached my dorm, the word had spread that Bud was dead, and everyone seemed convinced he'd killed himself. When I demanded to know why they'd say that, they claimed Bud's roommate, David, saw a suicide note on his computer monitor. That helped explain the questions the police officer kept asking.

"Refusing to believe Bud killed himself, I stood up for him, insisting there was no way. He was the same as always at lunch, and I wouldn't have been oblivious if someone I knew as well as I knew him was suicidal. How could I have failed to detect even the slightest hint? I was sure he didn't do it while high on drugs. We'd talked about that. He swore he'd never touched anything. He believed it was too big a gamble, in light of his aspirations, and I believed him.

29

"After my meeting with the police officer, I was tired and depressed. When one of the guys insisted that anyone with a brain knew Bud killed himself, I lost it. I couldn't stand by while people so readily wrote off Bud's death. I went toe to toe with him and said there was no proof.

"He said I had to stop letting friendship cloud my thinking, and I shoved him. He shoved back. We ended up in a knock-down-drag-out fight, and no one tried to stop us. When we finished, he had a broken nose and a black eye, and I had a black eye and a fat lip.

"I couldn't sleep that night. My mind raced. Between wondering what happened to Bud down by the bluffs and worrying about his family, I wasn't handling it well. I couldn't imagine how his family was coping. I wanted to call and tell them what a wonderful person he was, but I was afraid that might make things worse.

"At daybreak, I went running. Ran as fast as I could, hoping by the time I got back to my room I'd pass out and sleep for at least a few hours. I never skipped classes, but classes weren't a consideration that day.

"Before returning to my room, I went to Bud's dorm. I had to. It may sound crazy, but I hoped to feel less upset—a bit of relief, if somehow I could sense his presence. The crime scene tape across his door struck me like a slap in the face. I leaned up against the wall near his door, and I couldn't move. I just stood there, trying to feel a connection with Bud.

"After I don't know how long, because time meant nothing, I actually felt him there with me, in spirit, and I felt a little better. I did that for several days, always after my morning run. Then I called the officer who gave me his card and asked about the status of the investigation.

"My question was met with a long pause, then he said the county sheriff's office took over the investigation. No surprise, he didn't sound happy. He said that was a typical problem with working for a smaller department with fewer resources.

"I commiserated with his having the case taken away after he did the preliminary legwork. In an effort to form a connection and learn more, I asked whether he ever considered moving to a larger department. He said, 'Family commitments make it difficult, if not impossible.'

"I told him that some of the guys at school are saying it was suicide, and I asked if that was the direction he had been leaning. He said it was too early to be leaning in any direction, but it was a very real possibility.

"Wishing him the best, I hung up, discouraged that law enforcement appeared to be focusing on suicide. I wondered how I could prove it wasn't true.

"Desperately needing to talk to someone who would understand what I was feeling, I called Dad. We spoke the night Bud died and close to every other night since. I knew if anyone could help me through this, that was Dad.

"After he spent about an hour trying to help me, he ended our conversation with a challenge. 'If you know Bud didn't commit suicide, Son, prove it.'"

Six

Intermission

"Speaking of your dad," Katie said, "when you told me how you helped Bud cope with his grandpa's death, that sounded familiar." She smiled warmly at Pete.

"Are you suggesting I am a clone of my dad? Like he programmed me?" Pete laughed. "Obviously, he taught me a lot. I've always admired him."

Katie nodded and said, "Okay, let's get back to the story."

However, Teddy had other priorities and decided to announce them. He began screaming for attention ... or more likely, for lunch.

Pete stepped around Benji, who was parked in front of Teddy's crib, looked down at the tiny bundle, and smiled. Pete couldn't help smiling each time he looked at his son, and holding the little guy always gave him a warm, tender feeling.

Teddy stopped crying as soon as he saw his dad. Pete glowed at what he read as an endearment. He felt happy and contented every time Teddy smiled at him, despite having heard that, when a baby that young smiled, it's just gas.

Katie moved to her recliner in the family room, preparing to nurse Teddy.

Pete handed her their son, sealed the delivery with a kiss, and said, "I'll fix lunch. Soup?"

"If you mean the leftover liver dumpling, that would be great." She nodded.

The first time Pete mentioned this family favorite, she'd wrinkled her nose and looked at him like he was crazy.

When he told her Grandma Jackie gave him the recipe, she cautiously agreed to try it. Grandma Jackie was known for working miracles in the kitchen.

He told Katie that the first time Grandma Jackie asked if he'd like to help her make it, he shook his head and told her he hated liver.

She'd predicted that wouldn't matter—that he'd like it anyway. And she was right. Grandma Jackie got the recipe from her mother-in-law, Magdalene Schmitt, more typically addressed as Maggie.

According to Grandma Jackie, Maggie did little measuring. That made her nervous about how her first attempt would taste, but each time she made it, it was delicious.

Although Pete continued to avoid liver in any other form, he relished this traditional German soup called *leberknödel suppe*. It was made with beef broth and contained dumplings made from ground calves' liver, flour, baking powder, milk, an egg, and several spices.

The first time Pete tasted it, he noticed that the dumplings tasted a bit like liver. But they were so delicious, he didn't mind. He'd regularly asked Grandma Jackie to make this soup for them.

Katie loved it too, despite her dislike for liver.

While the soup simmered, she finished nursing Teddy, then she and Pete spent a half-hour playing with, doting over, and talking to their son.

Katie wanted to take a quick shower, and Pete took Teddy back to the nursery, changed his diaper, and rocked him to sleep. As soon as she heard Pete stop singing to the baby, Katie dished up the soup and set out a plate of saltines, a mug of coffee for Pete, and herbal tea for herself.

"I think Teddy's gaining weight," Pete said as he joined Katie at the table. "Soon we'll have to get him larger diapers and onesies."

"And the next thing you know, he'll be in college," Katie responded with a laugh.

"Hold on." Pete chuckled. "Let's not rush this."

"Besides, you have a lot to do in the meantime," she added.

Pete agreed, "Like building a swing set, assembling a trike, then a bike, working on his fastball ..."

"And finishing your story," Katie added with obvious enthusiasm. "I hate to be such a slave driver, but now that we have some time ..."

Pete laughed. "A guy can't get a minute's rest around here." Then he grasped Katie's hands, looked in her eyes, and said, "Before I continue, Katie, it's only fair to tell you that my first wife, Andrea, plays a significant role in some of the upcoming parts of this story. If, knowing that, you want to change your mind, I understand perfectly."

Katie kissed him and said, "I'd love to have a chance to get to know more about her, but will talking about her drag you down?"

"Not anymore," Pete said and shook his head. "Okay, Part Two."

SEVEN

Bud's Funeral

"**I** was determined to attend Bud's funeral for him and his family ... and for me. I figured I could take a Greyhound bus, but first I had to find out about the arrangements. I had an idea. I knew, from spending time with Bud, that he respected and admired his advisor, Dr. Richmond, the chair of the Computer Sciences Department. I hoped that went both ways, and Dr. Richmond planned to attend Bud's funeral. Both were true, so I asked if I could ride along with him and said I'd gladly pay for the gas. Happily, he said that not having to make the trip alone was payment enough.

"Because the family couldn't make the arrangements until the sheriff released Bud's body, the funeral was about three-and-a-half weeks after he died. I have no idea how they got him back to Madison. Much as I'd like to know, I couldn't ask the family.

"Early the morning of the funeral, Dr. Richmond picked me up in front of my dorm, and we spent the trip reminiscing about Bud. I knew that, having stayed abreast of computer sciences literature, Bud was familiar with all the articles Richmond had published. The fact he was the chair of their computer sciences program was the reason Bud decided to go to St. Jerome's in the first place. Dr. Richmond smiled when I shared that.

"He talked about the types of computer programs he and Bud developed together, and those they were working on when Bud died. He said he wasn't certain he'd have completed many of them without Bud's efforts. He didn't know of another professor or student with Bud's critical thinking and computer expertise. He said, 'Ours was a true synergistic relationship. Our combined efforts were greater than the sum of our individual efforts.'

"I told him how Bud and I met and about Bud becoming the valued statistician for the baseball team. And he told me how much Bud loved finally finding a home at St. Jerome's, thanks in part to our friendship.

"We arrived in Madison in time to catch the last fifteen minutes of the visitation, prior to the funeral Mass. I was disappointed to see the family decided on a closed casket. After more than three weeks, I hadn't got past believing Bud's death was some kind of mistake, and he'd be sitting at our usual table the next time I walked into The Commons. At more lucid moments, I wanted to see a placid, bruise-free face. I wanted to know he hadn't suffered.

"I walked up to the coffin, choked back tears, bowed my head, and said a prayer that Bud was in a far better place and reunited with his grandpa. When I turned around, right in front of me stood a guy who looked just like Bud. I almost grabbed and hugged him. Had I been right? Was this a horrible joke or terrible mistake?

"'Pete Culnane?' Bud's lookalike asked. He sounded a lot like Bud, but his voice was a bit deeper.

"'Win?' I asked. And he nodded and gave me a big hug. His body felt stiff and tense ... all knotted up. He thanked me for coming and said, 'Bud thought the world of you. He told me how you met and that he liked hanging out with you. Said you included him in stuff. He especially appreciated being able to hang out with the baseball team. Having a friend like you made college much better for him.'

"He continued, saying, 'I hear they're still looking at his death as a possible suicide. I can't believe it. He wouldn't kill himself, would he, Pete? If so, why? Did he say anything to you? Why didn't he call me, Mom, or Dad if he was that depressed? I talked to him at least once a week. What could possibly have happened in less than a week?' Tears were welling up in his eyes, ready to spill over.

"Then he apologized, 'Sorry for the interrogation, but I just don't get it. Losing him is bad enough. Claiming he may have killed himself makes it far worse. We're all overwhelmed. Mom can't stop crying. Dad has closed himself off. He won't talk to anyone. I understand from her husband that my sister, like Mom, can't stop crying and is unable to go to work. I feel like I'm in a fog, and nothing really matters anymore.'

"Aware of our surroundings, I whispered that I refused to believe Bud killed himself, that he wasn't depressed when I saw him just a few hours before it happened. And I watched Win's jaw, shoulders, and posture relax a few degrees.

"The funeral director's timing couldn't have been worse when he announced that everyone needed to head into the church. Win invited me to sit with his family, but I declined, figuring I should sit with Dr. Richmond, since I was there thanks to him.

"Win whispered, 'We have to talk more,' then he thanked Dr. Richmond for coming and for bringing me, and he asked both of us to sit with his family at the dinner, following the ceremony at the cemetery.

"Dr. Richmond and I stayed for the luncheon, but there wasn't room for us at the table with Bud's family. Later, when Win joined us, the environment was all wrong for me to ask the questions I needed his help in answering. I had to settle for exchanging phone numbers. I managed to tell him that I planned to contact the Sheriff's Office and, if they were still considering suicide, I would try to convince them there was no way.

"Win said he'd done that, but as best he could tell, his words fell on deaf ears.

"I said if anyone was wrong, it was the police and the people they chose to believe.

"Win sighed and told me how much he'd needed to hear that. He asked me, 'Can you help me prove he didn't do it? If I fail, it'll kill Mom and Dad. I'm not exaggerating.'

Katie closed her eyes, bit her lower lip, and sighed.

EIGHT
Getting Started

"Having promised to call Winston the next day, Sunday, I'd tucked his phone number into my wallet. Between the commitment I made to Bud after I learned his death was being investigated as a possible suicide, and knowing Winston was now counting on me, I felt weighed down ... almost overwhelmed. How could I prove I was right?

"I'd struggled with this even before Dad issued his challenge, but I'm embarrassed to say that in the last three-plus weeks, I had yet to attack his death head on. Instead, I'd spent every available minute gathering as much information as possible by listening and observing, while working to create my plan of attack. Before jumping into a pool of crocodiles, I wanted to talk to Winston and check my facts and assessments against what he knew and believed."

Pete looked thoughtful, then added, "Besides, I wasn't positive I knew everything that might have been bothering or upsetting Bud. Although I'd believed he would have shared those things with me, I had no proof. As the police officer told me, another perspective can be helpful.

"I also wanted to ask whether the police provided information to the family that wasn't available to people like me. I was afraid of going off half-cocked and, in the process, destroying my ability to prove Bud didn't commit suicide.

"After a few depressing hours at Bud's funeral and luncheon, Dr. Richmond and I dragged ourselves back to his car. We got situated for the long trip back to St. Jerome's, and I resumed creating a mental list of all the people I should talk to. Suddenly, it hit me. Here I was with Dr. Richmond's undivided attention, and he was an excellent resource!

"I told him about my conversation with Winston, and that Winston refused to believe Bud killed himself. Watching for a reaction, I asked, 'What do you think?'

"'Well, Pete,' I've thought a lot about that. When the police interviewed me, I told them it made no sense that he'd kill himself. I said Bud was in the middle of a project and totally enthused about the headway we were making. He was happy and content at school, in part because of his friendship with you, Pete.'

"I asked him, 'When was your last meeting with Bud?'

"'The day before he died. We met that Tuesday to discuss his class schedule for next year.'

"I asked him how far in advance he scheduled that meeting, wondering if it was so far back that Bud had abandoned his planning for next year by the time the meeting occurred. I wanted to know how Bud seemed when the meeting ended, whether he was distracted, upset, morose, depressed.

"Dr. Richmond told me the meeting had been scheduled roughly ten days beforehand. In the end, Bud was disappointed that he had to settle for a schedule that wasn't the one he wanted. As hard as they tried, and creative as they got, there was no way to fit all the classes he wanted into one semester. He was frustrated and wished he could clone himself, so he could take two classes simultaneously. Then he laughed it off, accepting the fact he wasn't the number-one consideration when class schedules are set. 'Are you doing what I suspect, Pete?' he asked. 'Are you looking for a reason Bud killed himself?'

"I shrugged and told him that for now, I was trying to determine what others believed about his death, and I asked if he was willing to help me.

"Dr. Richmond replied that failure to accomplish what Bud wanted wouldn't have been enough to drive him in that direction. Sure, he was driven, but he was a freshman. He had three more years to schedule and complete those classes. Also, Dr. Richmond told him that, if necessary, he'd arrange an independent study for him. Walking away from that meeting, Bud had worn a smile, and 'I keep seeing him that way,' Dr. Richmond said with a sigh. 'Furthermore,' he added, 'if he was suicidal, why did he waste so much of my time and his, striving to find a workable class schedule? It will take a lot to sell me on that.'

"So I asked if he could think of anything, anything at all, that was upsetting or depressing Bud. He thought for a minute. Then he described how, as he got to know Bud, he suspected something was bothering him and, the better he got to know him, the more convinced he became that it was true. One day, he came right out and asked Bud if there was something he'd like to discuss. Said he'd be happy to listen, and Bud had said maybe another time. He said Bud seemed a bit depressed at the time, but not *distressed*. It always seemed there was

41

something hanging over his head, weighing him down. He had reminded Bud a few times that he was ready to listen if he ever wanted to talk. Bud had thanked him and said he'd keep it in mind.

"Dr. Richmond said that a couple of months ago, Bud brought it up and said he'd finally worked through whatever it was. 'In fact, he said he'd accomplished it thanks to you, Pete.' He hadn't been moping all the time, just once in a while Dr. Richmond could tell something was bothering Bud. He'd seemed more prone to this whenever they discussed his summer project—a special assignment Dr. Richmond gave him to get into a class without taking one of the prerequisites. He knew from their discussions that Bud knew the material, but he had to be able to document it.

"Hearing that, I wondered if it was the project Bud said had kept him from seeing his grandpa on what would have been his last opportunity.

"I told Dr. Richmond that I ate lunch with Bud just hours before he died, and he wasn't depressed, anxious, or distraught. I couldn't imagine what might have happened in that short time to turn things around so dramatically. I asked if Dr. Richmond could think of anything.

"He scratched his jaw and thought for several seconds, then said that the only things he could think of that could happen that fast, without any buildup, would be something like someone unexpectedly threatening to expose him or go public with something that could harm or destroy him. He said 'Help me here, Pete. You're his age. Nowadays, what could that be?'

"I said if he was caught cheating or manipulating grades, he'd lose his scholarship. Dr. Richmond agreed that losing his scholarship might do it, but he didn't believe Bud needed to or would do either. He said he'd check just the same, since there would be a record. However, as Bud's advisor, he 'should' have heard about something like that before or at least shortly after Bud was confronted. He thought that, since Bud was fine at lunch, 'unless he's a phenomenal actor, any confrontation had to happen in the few hours between lunch and his death.' He'd check Bud's schedule to confirm, but he was fairly certain that he was in class most of that time.

"I told him that I knew Bud would never do any of those things. And if he planned on ending his life, he would not have promised to help me with a computer problem after practice. I couldn't believe that he'd reiterate it at lunch, if he wasn't going to do it.

"Then I had a revelation that I shared with Dr. Richmond. I would understand if Bud made up his mind and didn't want anyone to stop him. 'But then, how could he have been so happy at lunch?' I asked.

"Dr. Richmond pointed out that then the whole thing, from realizing the problem to concocting the solution all had to happen after lunch. And it had to be something huge. 'If it wasn't one of the things we've already pretty well discounted, he'd have had to do something like rape or murder someone, rob a bank ... or ...'

"'No way!' I responded about thirty decibels too loud. 'I knew Bud. He'd *never* do any of those things.'

"Dr. Richmond smiled and joked, 'Next time you're going to turn up the volume, can you please give me some advance notice?' Then, continuing to search for an explanation, he said, 'I don't think Bud was gay, but say someone threatened to *out* him.'

"I said that Bud had a girlfriend. 'I know he hadn't gone out much, but that doesn't mean anything. Lots of straight guys have trouble finding girlfriends.'

"Dr. Richmond said that might not stop someone from trying to hurt him by spreading the rumor.

"I said it wouldn't be much of a threat, when the guys on the baseball team and I would know it's a lie.

"Then he asked, 'What if his relationship with the woman he was supposedly dating was strictly platonic?' I assured him, 'I don't think you'd ask if you saw the way he looked at her.'

"He countered, saying, 'Maybe she just discovered she's pregnant?'

"I felt really stupid. I hadn't even considered that one. I asked, 'Do you think Bud's reaction to news like that would be suicide?'

"Dr. Richmond said, 'Actually, that would shock me.' If Bud was in love, he could see him asking her to marry him and working his tail off to make a go of it until he graduated. 'I couldn't imagine Bud leaving her to fend for herself and their child, abandoning both of them, washing his hands of the whole situation. In my opinion, that's what he'd be doing if he killed himself for that reason. Do you agree?'

"I agreed and said that wouldn't be the Bud I knew. Then I asked if he could think of anything else that might drive Bud to consider suicide. I refused to believe that's what happened, but thought to discount it, I might have to disprove all possible explanations. He said he'd think about that and get back to me.

"I said I knew Bud's class schedule, but he had access to the names of the professors. I told him, 'I want to talk to them, as well as other students in the classes he had between lunch and ...' I choked up and couldn't finish.

"Dr Richmond said, 'Good plan.' He promised to email that information to me on Monday, as well as whether Bud had been confronted by the administration about grade manipulation or anything else. By then, we were outside my dorm. I reached for the door handle, and he said, 'If you need a sounding board, don't hesitate to contact me, Pete. I'm in your corner.'

"I had one last question for him. 'After this conversation, Dr. Richmond, do you still believe there's no way he killed himself? Or do you think he might have succeeded in fooling those of us who knew him best?'"

NINE

First Steps

"'I'm convinced Bud didn't kill himself,' Dr. Richmond said. 'What could he achieve by going to such lengths to hide his emotional state and his intentions? Again, that's assuming we're both wrong and the reason for killing himself didn't surface until after the last time either of us saw him.'

"He believed the despair had to be extreme for Bud to reach that point, and he couldn't imagine that happening between lunch and the time he was found. In his experience, Bud wasn't one to just react. He didn't do things on the spur of the moment. He was a planner. He calculated the costs and benefits when it came to important decisions. He couldn't imagine him formulating and completing an act of suicide so fast ... even if he raped or murdered someone. And he didn't believe Bud ever did either.

"I added that, just as puzzling, was hearing that Bud apologized to his parents in the suicide note but didn't mention Winston. 'They were so close,' I said. 'As far as I'm concerned, the failure to mention Win is a sure sign Bud didn't write that note.'

"Dr. Richmond knew only that a note was found and asked me to tell him more about it. I said all I knew was what the guys were saying, and I couldn't guarantee it was true. Supposedly Bud's roommate, David, saw that the screen saver for his computer wasn't on and there was something on the screen. Since it was unheard of for Bud's screen saver not to be on if he wasn't there, David said he walked over and read the monitor. Purportedly, it said, 'Sorry Mom and Dad, I'm ending my life. Forgive me. I love you. Bud.'

"'David freaked after reading that. He ran and got the RA who read the message, then grabbed everyone he could find and searched the dorm and all the places Bud hung out after classes, starting with the library. Eventually, someone mentioned he liked to hike along the bluffs, and the RA took a bunch of guys there, looking. That's when they found him. Had it not been for that note, who knows when he'd have been found?'

"I added, 'I knew he liked to decompress by hiking along the bluffs. Had they not found him, perhaps I'd have looked there ... eventually. The question is, who typed that note? I intend to find out.'

"I asked Dr. Richmond if Bud's death was a topic of conversation among the faculty, and he said everyone wanted to know the story, yet many shied away from it ... like it was too uncomfortable a subject. After all, it was the first death to occur on campus.

"After saying goodbye to Dr. Richmond, while walking from his car toward my dorm, I thought about all we'd discussed and began prioritizing the people I needed to speak with. I decided to attack it from two different angles. One was that the events resulting in his death had been in the works prior to the day he died. In other words, it was premeditated. The other was that things happened without premeditation, and only started after I ate lunch with him for the last time. In both cases, to my chagrin, suicide remained a possibility, because I wanted to cover all the bases. I wanted to begin my investigation looking for the answers, rather than seeking to prove what I'd believed.

"I wanted to find the best order of attack, but I had no idea how to do so. If the people I talked to shared my interest and my questions with others, would that undermine the viability and reliability of my investigation? I was concerned about that and about mucking things up so badly I'd never learn the truth.

"Having to start somewhere, I placed Bud's brother Win, his girlfriend, and the professors whose classes he attended after lunch that Wednesday at the top of the list. I wasn't sure if I needed to talk to the friend who introduced Bud to his girlfriend.

"Having had a large lunch, we hadn't stopped to eat on the way back from Madison. It was only a little after seven. I didn't have Bud's girlfriend's phone number, so I called the friend who introduced them. No answer. It was rare for us to have cellphones, but lots of us had landlines in our rooms. We usually shared the monthly cost with our roommates and used calling cards for long-distance.

"By the way, Katie, every month Grandma Jackie sent me a letter that included an AT&T calling card. It might have been intended as a gentle reminder ... a bit of a nudge. With training, practices, and games, I didn't see much of her during the school year. Anyway, I used those cards to call her every few weeks to chat and let her know I hadn't forgotten her."

Katie smiled and nodded, knowing Pete was probably right about her ulterior motive—that sounded like Grandma Jackie. Gentle nudges were her modus operandi.

"I treasured those conversations," Pete said. "She always wanted to know if I still loved baseball, whether I liked third base any better, and how my classes were going. And she told me when to start looking for my next 'care package.' They also arrived about once a month and included her famous chocolate chip cookies, brownies, and homemade fudge. She kept me up to date on neighborhood news, the doings of my high school buddies, and her schedule. It seemed between bridge parties and visiting friends and family, she was usually out and about. Not much has changed, huh, Katie?"

Pete grinned. "I always looked forward to those conversations and, like now, the sound of her voice made me feel happy and content. Even then, I valued our special relationship ... our bond."

He stood and stretched before continuing, "Since Stuart's was the popular hangout Thursdays through Saturdays, I decided to head over to see if Bud's girlfriend Valerie might be there. If not, I hoped to speak with some of Bud's friends.

"I ran full out and managed to flag down The Link as it left for St. Elizabeth's. Then I walked the half mile or so to Stuart's and looked around. Wasn't surprised not to see Valerie, but I saw lots of my teammates and Amy, the person who introduced Bud to Valerie. Amy gave me Valerie's phone number, and I asked if she thought Bud killed himself. She nodded and said, 'They know he did. He left a note.'

"When I asked if Valerie accepted that, she said Val didn't want to, but had to once she realized the only other possibility was that someone murdered him ... 'and that could *never* happen at St. Jerome's. Besides, who else could write a suicide note on his computer?'

"I wanted to list the people, starting with Bud's roommate, David. Instead, I said the police were looking at it as only one of the possibilities. I also said I was positive Bud didn't kill himself.

"When she looked at me like I'd lost touch with reality, I asked, 'Why is everyone so willing to write it off as suicide?' She said the difference between me and them was they were willing to accept the 'unfortunate facts.'

"Knowing I'd achieve nothing if I lost it, I bit my lip and controlled my temper. I asked simply 'Who knew Bud better than me?'

"She said she heard about the fight, and everyone knew I was reacting with my heart, not my head.

"Getting nowhere, I changed the subject and learned that Amy and I were on the same page when it came to Bud and Val's relationship. In other words, it was going well, and they'd both shown lots of signs of being in love. She said it was always, 'Bud this and Bud that' when she and Val were together or spoke.

"Further evidence, according to Amy, was that Bud and Val got together every Saturday, and a few other times each week. 'Honestly, I thought she was head over heels,' Amy said, adding, 'Now, needless to say, she's inconsolable. Doesn't talk. Won't go anywhere. Looks like she cries all the time, and I think that's pretty well true.'

"When I asked if she had any idea what could possibly drive Bud to kill himself, Amy said it couldn't have anything to do with Val, because 'Val would never do anything to hurt him.'

"Thinking about my conversation with Dr. Richmond, I wondered if Val might be pregnant. Like

Dr. Richmond, I couldn't imagine Bud reacting to news like that by killing himself. Besides, unless he didn't find out until after lunch on Wednesday, wouldn't he have told me? I wanted to believe he would have. I didn't dare ask Amy. I figured she'd slap my face and storm away. Besides, if Val was pregnant, there was no guarantee she'd tell Amy ... or Bud, which brought up another question. I asked her, 'Do you know the last time Val spoke with Bud?'

"All she knew was that Val planned to see him that Wednesday night. Of course, that never happened. He died first. Val felt guilty and thought she should have known if he was despondent and the reason, and she should have been able to help.

"I began a series of questions with, 'Who was Val's boyfriend before she started dating Bud?'

"'Some guy back home.'

"'Where's home for her?'

"'Minneapolis.'

"'What happened to that guy?'

"'She broke it off when she came to St. Elizabeth's. She didn't want to be tied down.'

"'How did her ex take that? Do you know?'

"'Not very well,' Amy said.

"'Has he tried to see her since she came to St. Elizabeth's?'

"'She said he wanted to come up, but she didn't want to see him.'

"'Do you know his name?'"

"'First name only. It's Kennedy.'

"I asked if Valerie had spoken with Kennedy in the last few months. Said I wondered if Kennedy was jealous of Bud.

51

"She said he called a couple of weeks ago, her roommate answered, and Val refused to talk to him. He left a message for her to call him, but she didn't.

"After learning Val and Kennedy went to Bryn Mawr High School in Minneapolis, I asked if Amy could think of anything Val might have said to Bud that could have upset him.

"'First you didn't think he killed himself. Now you think it's Val's fault?' she demanded.

"'I'm positive he didn't kill himself,' I insisted. 'I'm just trying to get a feel for his emotional state.'

"'I already told you she'd never do anything to hurt him. Go find someone else to blame!' she shouted and stomped away.

"I figured I better work on my delivery *before* I met with Valerie. So I decided to hang it up for the day. The entire day had been too depressing to want to drag it out any longer. I caught The Link, alone, and headed back to St. Jerome's."

TEN

Bud's Girlfriend, Valerie

"**E**xhausted and feeling I'd achieved little on the positive side in my meeting with Amy, I dragged myself to my room, flopped down on my bed, and passed out.

"Sunday morning, my mouth tasted like I'd spent the night sucking on a dirty sweat sock. While cleaning up, I contemplated whether it would be best to call Winston or Valerie first. Either might tell me things that could help steer the conversation with the other. Finally, after accepting the fact that going back and forth was getting me nowhere, on my way into church, I'd decided to start with Valerie.

"At school, I attended Mass at St. Jerome's Church—an old church, replete with stained glass windows. Masses where the choir sang, accompanied by the pipe organ, were my favorites. The two, in combination, always made me feel, not just hear, the music. The pastor was another bonus. He was a real person. He didn't preach fire and brimstone. He talked about the acceptability of being human and the importance of accepting others.

"Since I arrived at church with no time to spare, I had to wait until after Mass to get something to eat. I placed my breakfast order, courtesy of a vending machine, and spent an inordinate amount of time rehearsing my questions and responses to anything Valerie might possibly say. She was potentially my most important resource, and I was intent on getting it right. Then I dialed the number Amy provided. It was almost noon, so I figured there was no danger of irritating her, by waking her out of a sound sleep. Her roommate, Anne, answered.

"When I asked to speak to Val, Anne wanted to know who I was. That left me wondering if she was running interference for Val. I told her and was greeted with an icy, 'She's not here.'

"Transitioning into my role as an investigator, I asked, 'Is something wrong, Anne?'

"'What could be wrong?' she snarled.

"That clinched it. Something was definitely blocking my path to Val, but I decided to play innocent ... or dumb. I knew of no reason for Anne or Valerie to be angry or unhappy with me, so figured I'd said way too much to Amy.

"I said, 'I'm confused, Anne, I can't imagine what I might have said to irritate you or Valerie.' Then I threw in what I hoped would be the incentive. 'I went to Bud's funeral in Madison. Talked to his family. Thought she might want to hear about it.'

"She said that Valerie should be back after dinner and I could try calling then. Her tone remained cold, and she didn't offer to have Val call me.

"I decided to toss in what I hoped would be another incentive for Valerie to speak with me. 'Don't know if you're aware of this, I said, 'but I don't believe Bud killed himself. And I'm intent on proving I'm right.' Whether or not she agreed with me, if Valerie blamed herself for not keeping it from happening, I thought that might give her another reason to want to talk.

"Anne didn't respond, so I thanked her and worked on finding the best way to proceed. I decided to try to reach Val by phone a few more times. If that failed, I'd try camping outside her dorm—to the extent my schedule permitted. Unfortunately, with baseball, my time was pretty constrained.

"If that also failed, I'd find a way to coerce someone who lived in her dorm or plant someone there. I hoped with some help I could bribe the girlfriend of one of my friends. After all, Valerie could be a critical cog ... if not *the* most critical one ... in this investigation.

Listening intently, Katie then asked, "Why didn't you recruit your girlfriend, Pete?"

"Well, at the time, she was a freshman at St. Cloud State University. Due to the challenges I faced, I thought about swapping her for someone living in Val's dorm, but that left a bad taste in my mouth."

Katie quipped, "So glad her feelings were an important consideration for a Casanova like you."

"That's like expecting me to consider your feelings when I'm working on a case. No way! It's not happening." Pete had a twinkle in his eyes.

"It's only important if you want a place to park your hide after you hang it up for the day," Katie smirked.

"And you know the only place I want to do that, don't you?" Pete kissed an index finger and pressed it to her lips.

Katie laughed and said, "And you're lucky I know when you're handing me a line."

ELEVEN
Winston Callaway

"**B**ud's brother was my next priority. A baseball game delayed that call. I played all nine innings at third and went one for three at the plate, but my mind wasn't on the game. Afterwards, I was amazed I hadn't committed an error, nor had I struck out every time at bat. I figured it was a payback. I was doing everything I could think of for Bud, and in return he was helping me.

"Honestly, Katie," Pete gave her a hands-up shrug, "I still felt like I had some sort of connection with him, and I didn't have a better explanation. One ground ball and one line drive should have handcuffed me, yet I handled both no sweat. As soon as I could, I ran to my dorm, hoping my roommate wouldn't be there. I had to talk to Winston.

"I'd hoped to huddle with him before or right after the funeral. But in no time at all, it became obvious, due to the overwhelming number of people in attendance and the absence of places providing privacy, that couldn't happen. So I'd promised to call the next day—Sunday—today. He offered to call me. Said he didn't want me running up long-distance bills.

"I'd begged off, because I wanted to make sure I was alone when we talked. I didn't want my roommate or any of his buddies to know what I was up to. That was the first time I'd wished I had a cellphone. My needs couldn't justify the expense, and I didn't have the money. But I realized how much easier this investigation would be if I had one. Then it wouldn't matter if my roommate was in our room. I could just walk out the door and make a call ... or walk out the door and continue talking. And I could make a call without first having to enter the calling card number and my password. The benefits became clearer as the investigation progressed.

"I worked on a term paper while praying that one of my roommate's friends would call or stop by and drag him off to do something ... anything. There I was, multitasking, before I ever heard the term.

"Unfortunately, Scott didn't leave until his buddies came and got him for dinner. The good news was, while waiting for him to leave, I finished that paper, and it wasn't due until Thursday. So as soon as Scott and his friends' voices faded away down the hallway, I grabbed the phone, went through all the preliminaries, and called Winston.

"After apologizing for taking so long to call and determining he wasn't in the middle of dinner, I dove in. 'Tell me everyone Bud complained about, everyone who was causing problems, everyone he disliked or hated.'

"Win asked, 'Aren't you even going to say hello?'

"'Sorry, yes. Hello. I hope you and your family made it through yesterday.'

"He said it qualified as the 'day from hell,' but he didn't want to use up my minutes talking about it. 'All I'll say is, I'm glad it's over with, and we won't have to do that again. Now, when it comes to your question, I know Bud didn't like his roommate, but I assume you already knew that, didn't you?'

"'Yes, but tell me the reasons he gave you.'

"'He thought David was sneaky—thought he was accessing information on his computer and stealing his ideas, for starters. Unfortunately, he couldn't prove it. It was just a suspicion ... an inkling ... a hunch. The last time we talked, he was working on a way to bust the guy. Aside from David, a few guys teased him about being a computer nerd, but he grew accustomed to that while he was in grade school and high school, and I don't think he ever took it to heart. The guys with any sense at all did what Bud said you and your teammates did. They asked for his help when they were in a bind. I don't think he ever charged for his assistance, unless perhaps someone had treated him like crap. If that happened, he never mentioned it.'

"'Hey,' he wondered, 'do you think there's a chance he charged someone, they found out he was doing it for free for everyone else, and they went after him for that reason, Pete?'

"I said, 'Only if he charged a really hefty price,' and added that, even so, it seemed like a really flimsy reason to kill someone, 'unless you're a head case. But I guess you have to be a head case to murder someone.' I asked if Win had any idea how much Bud might have charged in a case like that, and he had no idea.

"So I asked if Bud would keep a record of that, and he said he'd be surprised, unless Bud was charging several people. Then 'he'd probably do so to insure he charged them the same rate each time.'

"'Did he ever complain about being picked on or harassed?' I asked.

"'No, but it happened so much in grade school and high school, it may no longer have upset him.'

"'Did he ever talk about transferring to another school?'

"Win said, 'Only before he met you, Pete. As I'm sure you know, he was quiet and had trouble making friends. He was pretty much a loner. I think he might have wondered if he'd find more friends ... fit in better ... at another school.'

"Hoping for some ammunition to prove Bud didn't kill himself, I asked Win what he'd learned about the cause of death.

"Win said they were told Bud died of suffocation, due to a fractured trachea sustained when he went off the bluffs and hit a tree or large branch neck first. His face was all cut up, but the mortician claimed he could make him look like himself. He failed miserably. By the time he'd finished, Bud looked terribly bloated. 'That's why Mom demanded a closed casket.' Win's voice broke.

"Hoping to move on to something less painful, I asked if Bud talked to him about his girlfriend.

"'Yeah, like every time we spoke.' Win sighed. 'I used to think he'd never have a girlfriend. He really liked Valerie. He told me he was in love, and I told him he didn't know her well enough to be in anything but like. He said to wait until I met her. Said once I got to know her, I'd understand immediately. Sorry to say, I never had that opportunity.' Win sniffed.

"I said I spoke with Val's roommate, but hadn't yet talked to Val. I told Win, if she was dumping Bud, it might have sent him into a tailspin. But her roommate said she's 'devastated.' If Val was dumping Bud, I couldn't believe he didn't tell me immediately.

"Win agreed and said, 'Had she dropped him, I think Bud would have called me or spoken with you. Besides, he always thought through everything. He'd never react so radically that fast. You said he was fine a few hours earlier, right?'

"I agreed and asked if Bud somehow blew a test or his internship with Microsoft, in case he told Win but not me. He was confident neither had happened.

"I asked, 'Did the police or the university give or send you Bud's computer?'

"'If so, I haven't heard. You don't suppose my dad reacted without thinking and threw it away, do you?'

"I explained I didn't know the procedures the university or police follow, but I thought Bud's things, including his computer, would all be given to the family.

"Then I asked, 'What about his clothes and shoes?'

"'If they spoke with Dad over the phone, he may have told them to just toss everything. Thus far, he hasn't been able to deal with anything relating to Bud's death. And unfortunately, unlike Bud, Dad tends to react first and think later.'

"I told him it might help to know more about Bud's stuff ... about everything he held onto. There could be something that would give me ideas about how to proceed. He might have had notes or even threats he received.

"Win promised to see what he could do. He hoped if someone was contacted about Bud's things, it was his mom, not his dad. He believed that way there'd be a better chance those things still existed. Said he'd talk to both of his parents and get back to me.

"I thanked him and said I'd wait to hear from him. Told him that in the meantime I'd keep trying to reach Bud's girlfriend and speak with everyone else who might have information or be guilty. He thanked me and said, 'I know Bud is so happy that you're investigating his case.'

"I was reaching to hang up the handset when I heard Win yell, 'Wait! Pete?'

"'Did you say something?' I asked.

"'Yeah. So glad I caught you. I just thought of someone who hated Bud, but we're talking almost a year ago.'

"He told me that Bud was the valedictorian in high school, but barely beat out another student. That student's family was furious. They claimed her schedule was more demanding than his, her participation in extracurricular activities ought to carry some weight, and she was a better person. They even claimed it was sexist.

"Win said that their request for a formal review got them nowhere, and her dad and brother filed some kind of protest. They walked past Bud at graduation, casting aspersions, but Bud had figured that was the end of it. Just the same, Win wanted to bring it to my attention. He said her name is Abigail Bellingham and her brother is Murray.

"He added, 'By the way, Bud and the Bellinghams went to Edgerton High School. Because of having to deliver that speech, I've always believed he'd have gladly handed the award over to Abigail. He *hated* public speaking. He'd probably have given it to her anyway. He wasn't into the recognition game. All he seemed to care about was conquering a challenge.'

"That's when I realized I hadn't asked about Bud's phone. Specifically, who paid the bill, Bud or his roommate?

"'Bud,' Win said. I asked if he knew whether the bills list the numbers where incoming calls originate, and he had no idea.

"I'd hoped so. Even if the call lasted only long enough for Bud to answer and the caller to hang up, I wanted to see the last several bills. Who knew what they'd reveal?

"Then I asked, 'Did Bud get high school yearbooks?'

"'Yeah, but I'm not sure he ever looked at them. I'm almost positive he never had anyone sign his. Didn't want anyone messing them up.'

"I asked if Murray was now a senior at Edgerton. Win assumed so, but didn't know. Next I asked him to try to find pictures of Abigail, Murray, and their dad, suggesting he might find all three in Bud's yearbooks. They might come in handy.

"I think he was beginning to feel overwhelmed, because he definitely wasn't enthused with my last request. Even so, he said he'd do his best to find something.

"I thought of something else, hesitated for a second, then asked if he knew that Bud liked to walk in the woods, along the river bluffs. He did. Win said Bud was hooked on it as a way to relax. In response to another question, he said he didn't think Bud ever shared that fact with anyone, with the exception of me.

Pete shrugged. "After that, we disconnected. I think Win was relieved that I didn't dump anything else in his lap."

"Well, Pete," Katie teased, "you do get pretty intense when you're on a case ... or a mission."

TWELVE

Valerie Sanborn

"That was a lot to digest, I thought after talking to Winston, and my investigative workload was growing at an alarming rate. Glancing at my watch, I discovered it was only 5:30. If I caught The Link, I might be able to intercept Valerie on her way back to her room after dinner. Speaking face-to-face continued to be a priority, because I believed it was far more difficult to sell me on a lie that way.

"Figuring I had a spare minute or two, I tried calling her first. After all, it might go better if she was prepared to see me. Besides, I'd save a roundtrip to St. Lizzie's if she wasn't there when I arrived. Yes, I knew giving her a heads up about my arrival might backfire by insuring her absence, but ... When Val answered the phone on the fourth ring, I almost dropped the handset.

"'Val,' I gasped, 'this is Pete.'"

Pete shook his head and said, "I was the picture of cool, calm, and collected."

Katie chuckled.

"Val said, 'Anne told me you called. She suggested I do everything possible to avoid you. I'm not sure why she dislikes you so much. She refused to tell me what you want ... assuming you told her.'

"'I know you're having a tough time dealing with Bud's death, Val. Me too. I don't believe he killed himself. I saw him a few hours before he died. He was happy ... excited about seeing you that night. I can't stop thinking about him. I can't let go of this until I get some answers. I'm hoping you'll help me. If I come over, will you meet with me, Val? Please?'

"She shrieked, 'Are you suggesting someone killed him?'

"I said I had to leave right then to catch The Link and asked, 'Can I see you, please? I promise to leave as soon as you ask.' I knew that last statement was a gamble, but I was afraid she was going to tell me to get lost.

"'You *promise* to leave as soon as I ask?'

"I crossed my fingers and said 'Yes.'

"We agreed to meet in front of her dorm. And once again, I had to run full out to reach The Link in time.

"When I got on, the driver said, 'You know, with a little planning you could avoid having to test your lung power every time you want a ride.'

"I laughed, grateful for a touch of humor at a stressful time, and thanked him for his concern for my well-being.

"After plopping down on a seat, I thought about and dreaded my meeting with Val.

"I found her sitting on the curb in front of her dorm, looking lost. Feeling a warm rush of relief, I realized how nervous I'd been that she wouldn't show up. This was the first time I'd seen her since Bud's death, and tears streamed down her cheeks the minute she saw me.

"Bent on passing for the strong, controlled type, I fought to choke back my tears as she ran up, put her arms around me, and shook with sobs.

"She told me she was sorry, and she said she knew how close Bud and I were. 'How can you look so put together?' she asked. 'Is it because you're a guy? What am I going to do without Bud?' Thankfully, in that position, she couldn't see the tears I was holding back.

"We walked back and forth, arm in arm, along the northern border of the campus, talking through our tears. By then, I was doing no better than Val at controlling mine.

"Still seeking the truth about Bud's death, even if it was the last thing I wanted to hear, I asked if she thought she and Bud might have been drifting apart.

"She stopped, stepped out in front of me, and stared me down. 'Why would you ask that?' she demanded.

"I said I was trying to cover all the bases, and she asked if Bud had suggested anything like that. I explained the opposite was true, which, of course, produced another burst of tears.

"Then I asked if he seemed unhappy, depressed, withdrawn, or more distracted the last few times she saw him."

"'If anything,' she said, 'the opposite was true, and for the last few weeks, it seemed he was always smiling.'

"I'd noticed that too. He was no more talkative than normal, but a smile was usually plastered across his face. I wished I'd been nosier and asked why he was so happy. I figured it had something to do with Val, and he'd tell me when he got around to it.

"Then I asked if he'd been more nervous, anxious, or quieter, trying to think of all the emotions he might display if he thought someone was after him.

"She shook her head. So I came right out and asked if he seemed concerned about anything. School or anything at all.

"'No, Pete. Nothing.'

"I asked if she ever saw him glancing around or over his shoulder, still wondering if he'd been afraid.

"She insisted none of those things happened anytime they were together. She said they got together the previous Saturday and the Monday before he died. Then she told me about waiting to hear from him the night he died. She'd expected him to call before dinner, because they were getting together afterward and needed to set the time and location. Right after dinner, she tried repeatedly to reach him, because he hadn't called as planned. After several unanswered calls, she called a guy she knew who lived on Bud's floor and got the news.

"She started sobbing, and I put my arms around her, until she calmed down and relaxed a bit.

"Based on what she said, I was more convinced than ever that Bud didn't kill himself. Setting aside everything else, he could *never* do something that cruel to Val. I asked if she could manage a few more questions, and she nodded somberly.

"I attacked my questions from another angle. After all, someone out to get rid of Bud might not reveal their intentions to him. I asked Val about her last boyfriend and got the same answer Amy provided. They broke up before she left for St. Elizabeth's. No, he didn't take it very well, but all seemed fine until Christmas break. Then he showed up at her parents' a couple of times and begged her to get back together. She was glad to escape back to St. Lizzie's. His name was Kennedy Lansing, and he was enrolled at St. Cloud State. Val was thankful he didn't have a car, because St. Cloud was just a little more than an hour south. He called a month or so ago, left a message for her to call him, but she never did. She didn't have a picture of him, and she didn't bring last year's yearbook to school with her.

"Val said her older brother, Keith, was a junior at St. Jerome's, and he was one of Bud's fans, because Bud solved his computer issues at least twice. I'd already heard about Keith, courtesy of Bud.

"Next, I asked if she and Bud ever went walking in the woods at St. Jerome's. On campus, the only way to the bluffs was through the woods. Without coming right out and asking, I wanted to know if she knew he spent time along the bluffs every day.

"She shook her head and said he might have been protecting her from the wood ticks. She didn't mention the bluffs.

"Returning to more comfortable ground, I asked whether anyone ever expressed an interest in her, while she and Bud were together.

"'If so, they were certainly surreptitious,' she said, 'because I never noticed.'

"Striving to cover all the bases by returning to the unfathomable possibility of suicide, I asked if Bud had a typical Wednesday afternoon schedule.

"She nodded and said he was definitely a creature of habit. After lunch, he had two classes, then returned to his dorm and spent the time until dinner on homework or computer projects. She said she didn't understand computers enough to repeat the way he described it. She only knew it had something to do with computer security.

"There was still the question I'd avoided and wanted to ask, but I'd be treading on mighty thin ice. It related to whether she was pregnant. Lacking a better approach, I clumsily asked if Bud had been getting less affectionate.

"Once again, Val stepped out in front of me and red faced asked, 'Getting a little personal, aren't you?'

"I think I blushed. I remember my face felt like it was on fire. I think she knew exactly what I was asking. Anyway, all she said was, 'I plead the fifth.'

"In retrospect, I'm surprised that statement wasn't accompanied with a well-deserved slap in the face.

"After apologizing for being such a clod, I walked her back to her dorm and took off—trying to put as much distance between us as possible as fast as I could."

Katie couldn't stop laughing as she hugged him.

THIRTEEN
Bud's Professors

"**H**aving bungled the conclusion to my meeting with Valerie, I worried that I might have made her emotional state even worse. You could say I kicked myself all the way to The Link, but that would qualify as the understatement of the decade. It took the trip back to St. Jerome's, plus a five-mile run and a call to my girlfriend to begin calming down.

"Andrea and I had started dating at the end of the previous summer—just before I headed to St. Jerome's. Other than over Christmas break, we saw little of each other due to classes and baseball. Add the fact we were about seventy miles apart with no transportation; I'm sure you get the picture.

"For that reason, it didn't require a radical adjustment when most of my spare hours were dedicated to my investigation. Surprised to hear from me, Andrea spent about ten minutes telling me that I was only half as big a jerk as I thought." Pete smiled and shrugged.

"After laughing my way through our conversation, I felt significantly better."

Katie laughed at that and shook her head.

"Still lacking a plan of attack, I didn't mention Val's former boyfriend, who also went to St. Cloud State. While getting ready for bed, I planned the next day. With four classes and practice, my Monday schedule was pretty full. I decided to use my lunch break to check for Dr. Richmond's email and connect with at least one of the professors Bud had seen after lunch on the day he died.

"Grabbing something out of a vending machine for lunch was no sacrifice. After Bud died, my lunch break transitioned from something I looked forward to, to something I dreaded and often skipped. Following my last pre-lunch class, I ran to my room, checked my email, and smiled with relief when I saw one from Dr. Richmond. I breezed through it and grabbed the books for my next two classes.

"Bud had a chemistry lab after lunch, then philosophy. In those days, since St. Jerome's was a Catholic institution, at least one theology or philosophy class was mandatory. Lucky for me, both of Bud's classes were in the same building, and I hoped one or both professors would be in their classrooms, prior to their class.

"One hit. One strike out. I found Dr. Newport, the proctor for Bud's chemistry lab. He looked at me inquisitively when I walked into the lab. When I said Sterling Callaway was my good friend, he shook his head and said, 'What a terrible waste. Why would someone with all that talent and ability kill himself?'

"I answered by asking if he thought Bud appeared depressed or suicidal the last time he saw him.

"He said he could never have predicted it from the way Sterling acted that day ... or the few preceding weeks. Bud smiled so much, he'd wondered what he was up to. He'd noted that on Bud's last day, he seemed excited about something. 'I never found out what, but it was a positive type of excitement, not nervousness or depression or anything negative. Sterling was a quiet guy, not prone to small talk. In fact, he rarely spoke, except when answering one of my questions.'

"When I asked if Bud struggled in the lab, Dr. Newport shook his head and said, 'Sterling? Not a chance.'

"I asked if he had problems with any of the other students in the lab, and Dr. Newport said that, from what he saw, Bud was neither friendly with nor an enemy of anyone. He arrived and left alone. And the conversation between Sterling and his lab partners was pretty much limited to experiment-related exchanges. 'Never harsh and never particularly friendly.'

"When I asked for a list of the students in lab the last time Bud was there, he frowned and said, 'I'm sorry, but according to rule 4371, subdivision 13c, I'm not permitted to provide that information.'

"Before I could respond, he broke into a smile, checked his watch, and asked me to follow him to his office, where he printed the list and handed it to me.

"One last question occurred to me, as I turned to leave. Turning back to him, I asked if Bud completed his lab and left early that last day.

"He shook his head and said that Bud had finished early, but he spent the extra time talking with him. I didn't ask what they spoke about. I figured he'd tell me if he thought it relevant.

"On the way to my next class, I was smiling. One professor on my side of the tally, and twenty-one students to interview about his lab."

FOURTEEN
Strategizing

"With rare exceptions, running was now my standard pace. I ran from my last class to my room, scrambled into my practice uniform, retrieved the business card the police officer gave me, and decided to take advantage of my roommate's absence.

"Glancing at my watch, I realized I should be on my way to practice. Then for the first time ever, I decided, 'I'll get there when I get there.'

"My mission? Having spoken with Win, I decided to grovel for any added details I could get from law enforcement. When the officer who gave me his card was on the phone, I identified myself and asked if the police and sheriff still considered suicide a possibility. Seemed like a bad sign when all he said was, 'It's still an open case.'

"So I laid it on. I said with rumors running wild, it was impossible to know what was true. I told him a few facts might help me sort through things, accept what happened to Bud, get some sleep, and move forward.

"He responded, 'Sorry, son.' Then he added, 'Like I told you, we turned this case over to the county sheriff. All I can do is refer you to them.'

72

"Following a long pause, he added, 'Lots of people told us he was distraught over his grandfather's death. The most important was his own father.'

"I thanked the officer for his time and assistance and dashed off to practice. On the way, my mind jumped back and forth between my conversations with Win, Val, Bud's advisor, and his lab proctor. While immersed in this, it occurred to me I needed more of a strategy if I was going to succeed in uncovering what really happened to Bud.

"Meetings with his philosophy professor and the students in his last two classes were high on my list of priorities. Adding all the guys who lived in his dorm, his friends, and any enemies I could identify to my list of contacts made it daunting. But it didn't end there. I also had to find a way to get ahold of Val's last boyfriend, as well as the father and brother of the girl he beat out for the valedictorian honors.

"That's when it struck me. I sorely needed not only a cellphone, but wheels.

"While I should have been concentrating on baseball and practice, I strategized. In retrospect, the coach had to realize I was distracted. All I know is, he didn't say anything about it. It's possible, knowing I was having a lot of trouble with Bud's death, he let it pass. I was aware that his indulgence was unlikely to continue, and that added even more pressure to get to the bottom of this ASAP."

FIFTEEN
Bud's RA

"**R**elieved when practice finally ended, I returned to my dorm, dropped off my equipment, and headed over to Bud's dorm. The first thing I noticed was the absence of activity in the hallway. That supported my belief the chances were poor, at best, that anyone would have seen someone going to or leaving Bud's room that Wednesday. Hence, someone else could have surreptitiously placed the 'suicide' note on his computer.

"Granted, today was Monday, and there could be a significant difference from weekday to weekday, since many classes were four days per week, and the open day varied. I'd check that out later. One step at a time." Pete winked at Katie.

"I wanted to meet with the resident assistant on Bud's floor. As you already know, Katie, the RA is the upperclassman who gets a break on room and board for keeping everything running smoothly and protecting the facilities from destruction. There was also a priest living on each floor in the freshman and sophomore dorms. Perhaps they figured the RA needed some emotional ... or spiritual ... support." Pete chuckled.

"Bud had mentioned his RA only in passing, so I doubted he knew much about him. But I did know, thanks to Bud, which room was his and that his name was Everett Coates. I figured Bud knew who he was, thanks to the occasional meetings Everett conducted, but had little else to do with him. Just the same, I was anxious to talk to Everett, who launched the search after David found Bud's purported suicide note.

"It was a short trip from my dorm to Bud's, and I used the opportunity to pray that I'd find Everett. I wanted to get this investigation moving. Thus far, it felt like I'd accomplished little and, you'll be surprised to hear, Katie, I was growing impatient."

Katie laughed, rolled her eyes, and said, "You, Pete? Shocking!"

Pete grinned and resumed. "I figured Bud was smiling down on me when I found Everett in his room. Having seen Bud and I together from time to time, he knew who I was. He told me how sorry he was about Bud. Said he felt guilty Bud killed himself on his watch.

"I told him despite all the time Bud and I spent together, I hadn't a clue, so how could he know?

"He appeared to find a touch of comfort in that. It seemed premature, so I didn't say a word about my belief Bud had been murdered, and I didn't want to risk flavoring his answers to my other questions. So next, I asked how Bud got along with the guys on their floor and the rest of the dorm.

"He admitted not knowing much about Bud. The first semester, Bud seemed to spend all his time in classes, the library, or his room. He thought he studied all the time and didn't really talk to anyone, aside from a friendly 'Hi,' when passing anyone in the hallways. He mentioned Bud seemed happier after he and I started hanging around and after Bud got a girlfriend.

"The fact he didn't mention Bud's computer-related efforts told me the things he knew about Bud were based on observations ... not interactions. But that didn't stop me. I wanted to know how Bud's fellow residents reacted to and treated him, and the day-to-day environment on Bud's floor. All that would be gleaned primarily through observations. I hoped to benefit from Everett's strengths in that area.

"Everett didn't think anyone on the first floor really knew Bud. He also admitted he didn't know how Bud's roommate David felt about him and vice versa. To the best of his knowledge, they knew little about each other and cared even less. He figured they had nothing in common, from A to Z, and went their own ways.

"When I asked if anyone refused to respond to Bud's habitual greetings or muttered behind his back, the only person Everett mentioned was David. Even so, he thought it was harmless animosity between roommates who no longer wanted to share a room. He never heard nor saw any heated arguments between them.

"Then I asked for his best guess, regarding the percentage of residents and visitors to his floor who might go unnoticed. Everett closed his eyes, rubbed his chin, and told me those were 'difficult questions.'

"I said I only wanted a ballpark figure, and he laughed, knowing I was on the baseball team. I told him I had a vague idea when it came to my floor in my dorm and was trying to figure out whether that was representative.

"He relaxed a few degrees and asked if I was aspiring to be a statistician, and he grinned when I said, 'Too many numbers.'

"After silently rubbing his chin for what seemed like a long time, he answered that, in both cases, he thought maybe 10 percent of the people were seen, despite the fact many of the doors were ajar. He clarified that they may have known someone was out in the hallway, but not who.

"Continuing to pursue the possibility that someone other than Bud or David typed the note, I asked, 'During the spring months, when the weather is nice, how often do you open your window?'

"He pointed out the fact it was open at the time and said he did it a lot. He appreciated fresh air ... 'unless it was too hot or humid.'

"Seeing his window wasn't open very far, I asked if it opened any further. He walked over and raised it several more inches. I knew I could get through. But I was probably in the bottom 25 percent when it came to weight-height ratio. Everett was closer to average, so I asked if, with sufficient motivation, he thought he could crawl through his window.

"He chuckled and said it was funny I should ask. Freshman year, on a bet, he tried it. At the time, he was within a pound or two of his current weight. The payoff increased for every minute he did it under the five-minute time limit. He succeeded in two minutes and sixteen seconds. Said he was angry when the guys rounded up, rather than going with the closest minute. Said he had several scabs for a week or two, thanks to placing speed ahead of the impact on his body.

"I asked if anyone who wasn't part of the bet had approached him, wondering what he was doing.

"He said there wasn't really any foot traffic in the vicinity of his window and on his side of the building, and there wasn't much of a view out the windows. As a result, unless someone was staring into space, they weren't particularly likely to be looking out the windows

... much less at his window. The windows served more as a source of light and ventilation than a source of amusement, according to Everett.

"Then I got down to the hardest part of this meeting. I told him that rumor had it that he was instrumental in finding Bud, and I asked him to please tell me what happened. I explained that, 'So far, all I'm privy to is a flood of rumors, and many of them conflict.'

"Everett sighed, plopped down in his desk chair, and said, 'The whole thing was a nightmare. David came running down the hall, screaming my name. The first thing I thought of was someone trashed his room or his computer. I stepped out in the hallway, shook him, and told him to calm down and tell me what was wrong. He grabbed my shirt and told me to follow him. Then he turned and ran to his room. Because of the expression on his face, I was right on his heels. I was surprised when he stopped in front of Bud's computer, repeatedly jabbed an index finger at the screen, and yelled for me to read it. I did, and my heart sank. I tried to calm down and not jump to conclusions. It didn't help when David pointed out the time, 4:00. He said unless Bud was at a baseball game or practice, he was always there by then. *Always!*

"Everett continued, 'When I asked how he knew Bud wasn't at baseball, David grabbed a spiral notebook displaying the school crest and colors from Bud's desk and thrust it at me. He said Bud would never go to a practice without it, because he's the team's statistician, and he *always* logs the statistics and other team data in it.'

"'I tried not to overreact,' Everett's voice shook as he continued, 'I thought about giving Bud some time to show, but decided if the message on his monitor was a suicide note, we might be able to stop him. So we recruited everyone we could find and searched the dorm, then all other buildings. We didn't find him, so I asked everyone where else he could be. One guy suggested St. Elizabeth's and mentioned his girlfriend. Someone else said he often saw him heading for the woods by the river bluffs. About twenty of us headed for the walking paths through the woods. While we did that, David searched for a phone number to check with Bud's girlfriend. On our way out the door, I instructed him to calm down before he called, so he didn't scare her.'

Pete took a sip of his cold coffee and continued, "Everett described walking shoulder-to-shoulder, following the path. He took the position closest to the bluffs, thinking anyone intent on suicide would throw themself over the edge. Unfortunately, the early absence of snow meant there was nothing, other than a dozen steps, separating a walker from the edge of the cliffs. He said that ordinarily, because the park service was quick to plow the trails after a snowfall, there would have been a snowbank along both sides of the trail, and throwing oneself over the edge would require a more deliberate act. By taking the position closest to the edge, worst case, he hoped to protect the other guys from a gruesome discovery. 'After all, I was an RA and the oldest person in the group.'

"He said they moved painstakingly, intent on ensuring they didn't miss anything, including any clues. He feared the worst and dreaded what he'd see in the locations where the bluffs were the most treacherous, meaning the fall of anyone going over the edge wouldn't be broken by trees or bushes. 'As we passed an area where the bluffs were thick with trees fifteen or twenty feet below us,' Everett said, 'I spotted something that was bright white. The white stood out, against the browns of the trees and the greens of the budding leaves. If not for that, I would probably have missed it. I stopped and jockeyed around, trying to get a better look by assessing the view from every imaginable angle.'

"'Noticing I'd stopped and wondering why, everyone did likewise, gathered around me, and stared in that direction. One guy whispered that it could be one of Bud's Nikes, and my heart sank. Someone else mentioned he was amazed by how white those leather Nikes always looked, like Bud polished them every single day. Someone had a cellphone and called 911. By then, I was almost positive that what we saw was a shoe, even though we couldn't see a person attached to it. I began hoping someone threw it over the cliff for some crazy reason, and they wouldn't find Bud in that tree.'

"Everett had no idea how long it took for the rescuers to arrive and figure out someone was tangled in the trees. By the time they knew that, he felt like he was going to heave. After giving the EMTs his phone number, explaining who he was, and requesting a report on the outcome, he went back to the dorm. Most of the guys left with him, but a few who could identify Bud had remained.

"Everett sighed and said, 'As you know, it was Bud. We were too late.' He shook his head and looked dejected.

"I asked how far that shoe was from the edge of the cliff, and Everett looked at me questioningly. So I clarified by asking if Bud could have landed out there by jumping off the cliff or if he'd have had to take a running start.

"Everett said, 'As I remember it, his shoe wasn't out that far. If he threw out his arms and jumped, I think he could have landed there.'

"I said, 'Say he was running and tripped. In that case, could he have landed there?' Everett thought that was possible, and his expression and body language indicated he found a bit of comfort in the possibility.

"When I asked what time they found Bud's shoe, he said 'a bit before five.' He knew that because he heard the church bells while returning to his room.

"Thinking it would ease his mind, I considered telling him I didn't believe Bud killed himself. But I had to be careful what I said to whom. If a fellow student murdered him, I didn't want to risk knowledge of my opinion diminishing my ability to uncover the truth. Unfortunately, that also kept me from huddling with him to find other ways someone could type a message on Bud's computer. Later, I hoped.

"Relieved to be almost finished, I asked for Everett's room number during his freshman year. I wanted to check the level of visibility for that room, compared to Bud's. Turned out, he was on the same side of the hallway as Bud, but Bud was down several rooms. In addition, unlike Everett's room, bushes did a decent job of hiding Bud's window in the seemingly unlikely event that someone was interested in observing that window ... or who might be going in or out of it.

"'By the way,' I said on my way out his door, 'where is David staying these days? He isn't still staying in his and Bud's room, is he?' Even if the police allowed it, I couldn't imagine anyone being able to do that.

"David spent the Wednesday night Bud died and the next night with Everett, since there weren't any open rooms at the time. Then he went home to Bemidji and hadn't returned to St. Jerome's. Everett didn't know if he'd ever come back.

"That complicated things. I hadn't spoken with David. Doing so now would be a challenge. Not only did I have to get to Bemidji, but to get straight answers, I probably had to find a way around his parents.

"It proved to be the least of my problems."

SIXTEEN
Digging For Answers

"**I**ntent on speaking with everyone I could find on Bud's floor, I went door to door. Either my timing was poor, or most people ignored my knocking. The strange thing was, this seemed like a good time to study. It was past dinner, and Stuart's wasn't an option on Mondays.

"I found a guy in the room across the hall from Bud's. He said he was under pressure to finish a paper, but would give me ten minutes. I hoped that would be more than enough.

"His name was Kyle, and I'd seen him occasionally when hanging out with Bud.

"I started by asking if he was there the afternoon Bud was found.

"'Unfortunately!' he confirmed and explained that he was studying for a test when David went screaming down the hall. The commotion became so great, he had to move to the library. Even the lounge on their floor had been out of the question. 'I felt bad,' he added, 'when I heard what happened and realized I should have been helping to find Bud.'

"When I asked for his take on Bud, he said Bud seemed painfully shy, and he stayed pretty much by himself ... until second semester, when he seemed more comfortable and happier.

"Then I asked for his take on Bud's relationship with David.

"Kyle frowned and sighed. He said he and David were friends, but they spent less time together these days. By way of explanation, he said before any of this happened, he knew David was in his room one afternoon and went over to talk to him. They weren't in the habit of knocking. 'After all, why bother?' he asked. 'We're all guys.'

"He was surprised to see David sitting in front of Bud's computer, typing away. David said he was in a hurry to send an email to one of his professors, and Bud was already connected to the network. So he decided to save time and use Bud's computer.

"'The thing is,' Kyle said, 'David wasn't sending an email when I interrupted. He was looking at what appeared to be a term paper. I couldn't imagine what legitimate reason he had for being on Bud's computer. Although Bud and I rarely spoke, I told him about it. I thought he had a right to know. I'd want someone to tell me if we were to switch places.'

"'Also,' Kyle added, 'Bud's screen saver should have been on. If it was, how would David know he was signed onto the network? Anyway, Bud was very appreciative. Afterwards, I sometimes heard him and David arguing in hushed tones. I felt kind of bad and wondered if I should have kept my mouth shut. I was sorry to have created a rift between roommates.' Kyle shook his head.

"When I asked how far back all of that happened, Kyle said it was a couple of weeks before Bud died.

"He hadn't shared the story about Bud's computer with the police. Figured he had no right to point the finger at David and make his life hell, when he had no reason to believe it had anything to do with Bud's death. I wondered how many other students did something similar.

"I didn't let on that I knew David had gone home, before asking if he'd spoken with him after Bud died. He said it was almost ten when he returned from the library, saw the police, and heard about Bud. He saw David the next day, but they were both rushing off to class and didn't have time to talk.

"The next time he saw him was at dinner on Thursday. He said David looked awful and ate little if anything. He told him how sorry he was, and David just frowned and shook his head. Kyle offered to buy him a beer at Stuart's, thinking that would give them a chance to talk, but David just shook his head again. He looked like he had just lost his last friend. Kyle told him they'd do it another day soon, and David nodded.

"'The next I knew,' Kyle continued, 'he'd split, ran home. Based on what I heard from the other guys, he didn't discuss it with anyone. He just took off, like he was running for his life. When I heard that, I can't tell you how glad I was that I didn't sic the cops on him. That would only have made things worse. I sure hope he manages to get his head screwed on before he blows the whole semester.'"

Katie interjected, "This is getting interesting—so many possible suspects. And you behaved much the way you do now."

Pete smiled and continued.

SEVENTEEN
Father Joe

"**M**onday night, I spoke with Father Joe, the priest who lived on Bud's floor. I opened by asking how well he knew Bud, and he said far better in the last weeks of Bud's life than previously. I must have looked shocked, when he told me Bud came to see him five days before he died.

"I stood with my mouth hanging open. After what seemed like an eternity, Father Joe said the Friday afternoon before he died, Bud asked him to hear his confession, and he was intent on it happening that afternoon. Of course, he was neither willing nor able to share anything Bud told him.

"I'll insert a sidebar here, Katie. It was thanks to that long, uncomfortable pause that I discovered the benefit of allowing a silence to persist—and to do everything possible to avoid being the one to break it." Pete chuckled.

"To insist on an immediate confession, I thought Bud must have had something weighing heavily on him. At least that would be the case if it were me. I couldn't imagine what would be that pressing for a guy Bud's age but contemplating that was getting me nowhere, so I forced myself to push it from current consideration. Father Joe helped me do that when he said he thought Bud also came looking for spiritual guidance. He wouldn't tell me anything more about it than that, but thought I should know that much.

"I knew priests were sworn to secrecy when it came to anything anyone told them in confession, but I didn't know why he couldn't say more about the spiritual guidance he provided Bud. Just the same, I didn't think pointing that out to Father Joe would get me anywhere, so I asked for his take on Bud's interactions with the other students on their floor and around campus, in the event he'd observed him out and about.

"He told me what I already knew. Bud typically avoided others and seemed to say little to anyone, other than his friends. He never looked strangers in the eye, and he went to great lengths to avoid interactions with all but a few students. On the other hand, he was far more comfortable with the professors.

"As Father Joe showed me out, I stopped, looked him in the eye, and asked if anyone other than Bud was intent on confessing the day he died or later that week. I hoped to see some sort of reaction, showing that happened. He stood stone-faced—didn't even flinch. But he didn't say 'no.'"

EIGHTEEN
An Assist from Andrea

"Feeling a bit defeated after my meeting with
Father Joe and convinced I'd achieved all I
could hope for that day, I headed back to my dorm.
Pushing aside the homework hanging over my head, I
called Andrea, hoping she'd raise my spirits and help me
relax.

"Talking with her, I ran through a summary of the
developments in my investigation, then mentioned my
conversation with Father Joe. She suggested Bud may
have been seeking spiritual guidance about his
relationship with Valerie. I thought, but didn't say,
especially if she's pregnant.

"I asked if she could con her brother out of his car,
so I could use it the next weekend. Rick had graduated
from college the year before, and he lived and worked in
St. Paul. Last I knew, he was a chef at some prestigious
restaurant.

"Andrea knew I didn't have a car, and I explained
how important it was that I get to St. Cloud, Bemidji,
and Madison, Wisconsin, ASAP. Rick and I never hung
out together, but seemed to click any time our paths
crossed, so I hoped to barter with him.

"Andrea asked if there was anything she could do to help, since she was already in St. Cloud. That's when I decided to ask if, in the midst of the morass of freshmen, she would try to find one named Kennedy Lansing. I narrowed it down, but barely, by adding he was from the Twin Cities and might live on campus.

"She said she'd try, and when she asked what I wanted her to do if she found him, I said I needed to know whether he was in St. Cloud between 3:00 and 4:00 the Wednesday Bud died.

In response to Katie's questioning look, Pete explained, "That was based on the fact it takes more than an hour to drive from St. Cloud to St. Jerry's. If he killed Bud at the earliest possible time, he couldn't get back by 3:00. He had to push Bud over the cliff no later than 4:55 or he'd have run into Everett and the others searching for him. In that case, he had to be on his way to St. Jerome's no later than 4:00. Either way, if Lansing did it, he had to be gone at least a part of the time between 3:00 and 4:00. To do it in so little time, he had to know where to find Bud and go right there. But how did he know Bud's schedule? Unless they'd corresponded and planned a meeting, how did he know where to find Bud? And everything had to fall into place perfectly.

"Andrea asked what would suffice, and I said the word of someone she trusted who was with him the entire time. We'd gone off on a tangent, so again I asked about borrowing Rick's car.

"She gave me Rick's cellphone number and said that, with a little encouragement from her, he might be willing to drive to St. Cloud and spend the weekend with friends. When I asked what it would take to get her to do that, she said, 'Invite me along.'

"I told her I would be sleeping in the car, assuming there was time to sleep. I had a lot to do in two days. She said that was fine, and she'd bring a bunch of food. So I tried another approach. I asked what she would do while I was talking to these people, and she said she could take notes.

"I explained how that might succeed in shutting down any meaningful conversations. So she pointed out that if any of them had a girlfriend, sister, or mother, she could talk to that person while I spoke with whomever. 'If you tell me what they might know that would help, I think you'll be surprised how much I can learn ... and share with you.'

"When Andrea said that, I realized by doing so she might also eliminate an unwanted audience when I spoke with whomever. That could significantly increase the chances of a meaningful meeting.

"We left it that she'd call Rick and tell him I'd call him tomorrow and why. I'd call her once I spoke with him. After hanging up, I hit the books. Studied until a little after midnight, doing the things I should have done after practice ... all things being equal. All things were, of course, anything but equal those days."

NINETEEN
Baby Steps

"**O**n Tuesday, in the early morning hours, I took a refresher course on the disadvantages of going to bed with something hanging over my head. Granted, Bud's death would hang over my head until I figured out who did it—or, far less satisfying and far more painful, that it was suicide.

"Fortunately, I found ways to divide the investigation into more manageable segments, and I usually succeeded in settling for completion of any of them. On Monday night, I slept maybe three of the six hours I spent in bed. I spent the rest of the time concocting ways to coerce Rick into loaning me his car, in the event he rejected my proposal. I also worked on a list of alternatives if that too failed.

"Everyone not readily accessible was a problem. If Rick loaned me his car, I had a lot to achieve in a weekend, and there was no guarantee I'd locate anyone on my list. So I thought about my options should any or all of them not be at home, at school, or wherever. I also tried to determine how long I could hang around each location, waiting for them. To keep it from getting too simple, I threw in how I'd locate Lansing at St. Cloud State, if Andrea failed.

"It would be easier and more efficient if I scheduled appointments, but I couldn't. Attempting that with the one who killed Bud would probably guarantee their disappearance. After all, I was just a college student looking for answers. I had no right to demand anything from anyone.

"After dragging myself out of bed, I ran. While running, I labored over how early I dared call Rick. I should have asked Andrea. Unfortunately, I didn't.

"If he was still a chef, that did little to narrow down his working hours. I figured, worst case, he was probably out of bed by 9:00. I decided to leave a cushion and call at 10:10, after my second class.

"You'll be shocked to hear this, Katie. During those classes, thoughts about that call had me totally distracted."

"You?" Katie laughed. "At least you've outgrown or overcome the inability to sleep when things are hanging over your head. Lucky thing. If not, you'd go days without sleep with every case you worked."

"It's just a matter of dividing it into manageable segments." Pete smiled.

"When I called, Rick was sound asleep. Turned out, he worked nights as the sous chef. He wasn't angry about being woken up, because he knew why I was calling. He told me he wished he could help but, unfortunately, he was taking part in cooking competitions the next two weekends. He said he was off Thursday and Friday and could only loan me the car those two days. Since I couldn't wait three weeks to search for these people, I said I'd make that work.

"I needed to clear that with the coach and several professors. Figured my professors would be more understanding, and I was right. The fact that Bud had been our statistician was probably the only reason the coach didn't blow up.

"Next, I called Andrea. She was still working on tracking down Lansing and reminded me there were more freshmen at St. Cloud State than the entire enrollment at St. Jerome's. She sounded mighty defensive, so I told her I knew it was a major undertaking and I appreciated her efforts.

"Anyway, she was willing to skip her last class on Thursday and her Friday classes. That way, she could pick me up about two o'clock on Thursday. I sighed when I realized that left little more than a day to find and meet with three people. I figured I had no choice but to postpone Kennedy Lansing. If all else failed and Andrea was unable to eliminate him as a suspect, I'd hitch a ride to Brainerd and catch the Greyhound to St. Cloud. I thanked her profusely, arranged our rendezvous for Thursday, and hustled to my next class.

"As soon as that class ended, I sprinted to the classroom where Bud's philosophy class met, intent on speaking with the professor after that class adjourned. Failed for the second time. The room was empty. Then I saw a note taped to the door. It said class was canceled and displayed the assignment for Wednesday. So far, my day felt like a bust.

"I hurried over to practice, hoping to salvage something of my day by speaking with teammates and coaches. The opportunities proved scarce and brief.

"Not surprised that everyone was sorry about Bud's death, but I was surprised that the coaches seemed to feel a deeper sense of loss than some players. It appeared the players least affected, emotionally speaking, were often those Bud tried the hardest to help. I didn't get that information from them. It came from members of the team who'd heard them muttering about Bud taking all the fun out of the game or screwing up their swing, batting average, earned run average, you name it.

"Supposedly one player, who remained unidentified, complained that Bud hurt his performance, because he was up against more than the pitcher when at the plate. He felt Bud scrutinized his every move. Unbeknownst to me, Bud had become a scapegoat for some players. I wondered how aware he was of this and worried it had taken the joy out of it for him. Would he have told me? I thought so, but I wasn't certain. It troubled me that I'd been oblivious to all this.

"Then I realized that due to my friendship with Bud, those guys wouldn't have said any of those things if I was within earshot. Just the same, in my mind, that didn't give me absolution.

Pete sighed. "That day took a lot of the fun out of baseball for me, Katie."

For Katie, it felt like Pete was reliving those days through the telling.

TWENTY
Additional Revelations

"**H**aving arranged for a car and aware of the time constraints, I was under pressure to do everything possible to ensure the success of our trips to Madison and Bemidji. The only thing I could think of was creating a reason for David, Bud's roommate, and the Bellinghams, the family of the girl Bud beat out for the valedictorian award, to want to see me as much as I wanted to see them.

"I figured the Bellinghams must know about Bud's death—either because one or all of them killed him or thanks to the local media. In light of the link between Bud and the three of them, I wracked my brain, trying to come up with something. Anything.

"The best I could do was the sash Bud must have worn over his gown, during the graduation ceremonies. I assumed that was standard practice. At least the valedictorian in my high school wore one.

"Believing Abigail should have received that sash, would getting it now be important to them? Did Murray, his father, and/or his sister lust after it? Or would offering it to them now make them angry?

"Could I offer it on the condition of meeting with me, then refuse to relinquish it? I knew I could not ... with one exception. If any or all of them killed Bud, I'd have no qualms.

"There was another key consideration in executing this plan. How sentimental was Bud's family? Based on my last conversation with Win, it seemed like his dad wasn't at all. How about his mom? In hopes of uncovering the truth, would they sacrifice that sash? For lack of a better choice, I had to ask.

"Or could I get a foot in the door if I told the Bellinghams that Bud regretted Abigail not being named his co-valedictorian?

"How about David? Knowing my link to Bud, would I be the last person in the world he wanted to see? How could I change that?

"I decided the RA on Bud and David's floor might be able to help. I found Everett in his room and asked if David left anything behind when he went home.

"Everett said there was nothing important, but he found a St. Jerry's baseball cap and a sweatshirt. I took them back to my room and thought about what would be more enticing. Decided, in light of Kyle's revelation about catching David at Bud's computer, I might have a better option.

"That evening, I grabbed a hamburger on the way from practice to my room. I didn't have time for a sit-down meal, and I wanted to spend the first alone time I had talking to Winston. I hoped he'd be available when I got a chance to call. If not, I decided I'd use the pay phone at the library and make as many trips as it took to reach him.

"Pay phones were nearly extinct by then. We'd pretty much killed off their food supply, while their predators multiplied, largely unchecked." Pete chuckled.

"I must have grimaced when I walked into our room and saw my roommate wrestling with his buddies. The room was a mess. There was junk all over the place. As soon as he saw me, Scott assured me they hadn't touched any of my stuff and said they were just leaving.

"I shrugged. After all, it was as much his room as mine. Besides, all I cared about was their departure, so I could use the phone.

"Winston wasn't home, and the pessimistic side of me began worrying it was a sign of things to come. My outlook improved when he returned my call before Scott reappeared. I told Win I'd be in Madison on Thursday night or Friday and asked about his availability. He gave me his address and promised to be there until I showed up. He also said he'd get a photocopy of the yearbook pictures of Abigail and Murray. He already had a newspaper photo of their dad—from his obituary.

"I cringed when I heard that and wondered if I dare bother the Bellinghams.

"Win didn't seem concerned about it when, without pause, he said Murray was a senior at Edgerton High School, and Abigail commuted to the University of Wisconsin–Madison.

"I opened my mouth to ask if he could possibly find out their dad's cause of death ... just in case, even though it probably had nothing to do with my investigation. You never know.

"Before I could ask, Win said he'd called several friends to see if any of them knew the cause of death. It took about a dozen calls before someone said she heard he committed suicide. If that was true, Win figured there had to be something about it in the newspaper. So he called the local branch of the library and asked to speak with a reference librarian. When connected, Win asked if he would search for any articles about the death of Stephen Bellingham, including any obituaries.

"'We struck gold,' he said. 'Bellingham died of a drug overdose. It was still an active investigation, but the police were leaning toward suicide. And before you ask, Pete, he died exactly two weeks after Bud.'

"I told Win he was amazing, that I was running and still couldn't keep up.

"He thanked me and said he'd also located and gone through some of Bud's stuff from St. Jerry's, including his journal. I was amazed to hear we both kept journals."

Katie smiled and said, "And you're refreshing your memories by looking at yours from your college days, aren't you? That's why you remember the details so clearly?"

"Busted." Pete chuckled.

"Starting with the most recent entry, Win was working his way back in time. He hadn't gotten far, but two things seemed particularly important. One was that Bud was certain his roommate was accessing his computer and copying some assignments. He was setting up a trap. If he was right and could prove it, he'd planned to report it to the professor.

"Wondering if David might have seen and read the journal, I asked if Win could tell me the kinds of things that were in the box or whatever that held the journal. He couldn't, so I asked the date on that entry. It was two days before Bud died. The other item dealt with the Trojan condoms Win found in Bud's stuff. Per the journal, Bud believed Val's brother Keith saw him standing in line at the bookstore to buy them. He wrote that he thought he had them well hidden, but the look on Keith's face scared him. 'If looks could kill,' the journal said. Seeing that expression, Bud had returned them to the display and left the bookstore. But that didn't stop him. Several hours later, he returned to the bookstore and bought them. The date on that journal entry was the day before Bud was murdered.

"Win asked, 'How well do you know Val's brother?' Might protecting his sister from Bud have been the motive?'

"'In 1999?' I asked, while wondering the same thing. I told him I'd be amazed, but said I didn't know her brother well enough to be sure.

"When I asked if Bud's journal mentioned receiving any threats, Win said thus far he hadn't seen anything indicating he had or was afraid of anyone. While that didn't eliminate the possibility, I thought if either was true, it should have been in the forefront of Bud's thoughts during his final days—hence in his journal. And he hadn't seen any mention of Kennedy Lansing.

"After getting the Bellinghams' address and phone number, I said I wanted to broach a delicate subject. Then I told him about my efforts to think of a way to guarantee a meeting with Murray and Abigail Bellingham. 'How would your family feel about sacrificing Bud's valedictorian sash?' I asked.

"Win assured me it would be worth it to them, assuming they were guilty, and I could prove it.

"I told him I'd do my best, but I couldn't guarantee anything.

"After a long pause, he said he'd be right back. A few minutes later, he said Bud also received a medallion on a ribbon with the school colors. It was far more important to them than the sash ... 'and easier to display.'

"In light of all the Bellingham family had been through, I was reluctant to bother them, and I hoped neither Murray nor his sister did it. If their dad did it, he'd already paid the price."

TWENTY-ONE
Efforts to Influence

"I had a couple of newsflashes while preparing to speak with Murray Bellingham. It was lucky Andrea was coming along. She could talk to Abigail while I spoke with Murray. That way, she could keep Abigail from interfering or overhearing what Murray told me before I spoke with her. Also, in light of all the miles we had to log, it seemed we needn't worry about sleeping arrangements. We were likely to have to take turns sleeping, while the other drove.

"Before calling the Bellinghams, I looked up the driving time from St. Jerry's to the Callaway home. It was just over six hours. If Andrea arrived on time, and that was almost certain, and if we left right away, we'd reach Win shortly after 8:00. I also mapped the route from the Callaways' to the Bellinghams'. That was another fifteen minutes. Best case, we couldn't reach the Bellingham's until a bit before 9:00.

"Keep in mind, Katie, this was way before GPS. I had to go online and use MapQuest. Then I had to print the directions, maps, estimated drive time, et cetera. Even so, it was far better than the huge paper maps people used to fumble with. It wasn't, however, as good

101

as the AAA TripTik Travel Planners Mom used to order whenever we went on a family vacation. Think how incomplete Teddy's life will be. He'll never experience the finer points of travel."

Katie laughed and said, "Like when you and your parents came over on the Mayflower, then traveled by oxcart to the Midwest? You're right, the poor little guy. Do you suppose he'll even have a chance to see a gas station? We should start taking pictures. I'll find my Polaroid and shop for film."

"I suggest you look for the film at antique stores." Pete smiled, then continued with his story.

"I was relieved that Murray was home, and I prayed for divine intervention in both this conversation and in the meeting I hoped to schedule.

"After explaining who I was and giving him my condolences and those from the Callaways, I told Murray that the Callaways had something for him and his family, and they asked me to serve as the go-between."

"'We don't want anything to do with any of them!' Murray screamed so loud I thought I'd have a ringing in my ear for a day or two.

"I thought about asking if he knew Bud died, but decided I needed to see his face when I did. So instead, I asked him to please give me just ten minutes of his time. I said I had a gift for Abigail from Bud, and I had to deliver it in person. Suggested if he didn't want to see me, perhaps I could speak with her.

"He must have held the receiver about a millimeter from his mouth as he yelled, 'Abby!' I figured I'd have to get fitted for hearing aids as soon as I got home. By the time she came on the line, I was fearing failure and sweating profusely.

"I said I was calling on behalf of Bud Callaway and his family. Intended to say more, but she jumped right in and apologized for the way her family had treated Bud. She said she knew how schools determine the valedictorian, and 'Bud earned the honor.'

"Those remarks convinced me she and her family knew about Bud's death. Did they find out the usual way or did they play a part?

"I asked if I could see her at about 9:00 the next night and said it meant a lot to Bud's family. I didn't mention the sash. Thought I might not have to offer it up to get the answers I needed.

"Abigail said if the Callaways requested it, she'd be happy to meet with me that day and time. Then a second later, I heard the dial tone. I didn't even have a chance to thank her. I tried to convince myself that her quick exit didn't carry any negative connotations.

"Since tomorrow's schedule was now set, I called Win again and told him I'd see him tomorrow, hopefully about 8:00.

"'Murray agreed to meet with you?' he asked. He sounded amazed.

"I explained I was meeting with Abigail and hoped she could account for her dad and her brother's whereabouts the day Bud was murdered.

"He said he'd have both the sash and the medallion ready for me. He and his family would like to keep one of the two, and they were happy with either.

"David was next on the agenda. I estimated, best case, the Bellinghams wouldn't throw us out after a minute or two. So allowing as much time as I thought we might need plus an hour, I went back to MapQuest and obtained our route from their home to Bemidji. The estimated travel time, with no consideration for traffic jams, accidents, pit stops, et cetera was seven-and-a-half hours. By then, I was a bit more realistic. Rather than taking turns driving and sleeping, I decided we should stop at a wayside rest and both of us sleep.

"If we left the Bellingham's at midnight, parked at a rest stop for eight hours and continued on, we should be to Bemidji no later than 4:30. I didn't think there was a chance we'd sleep for eight hours, but I was estimating worst case.

"If we spent two hours with David—another unlikely event, we'd be back to St. Jerome's by 8:00 Friday evening. I could buy Andrea a quick dinner, and she'd easily make it back to St. Cloud by 10:00. Again, this was the worst case, and I thought Rick should be good with that schedule.

"Thanks to all the stress triggered by my call to the Bellinghams and all the plotting, my face and shirt were soaking wet.

"Since David knew me and my relationship with Bud, I wondered what the chances were of a reception similar to the one I got from Abigail. As much as I wanted to take a break before making that call, the looming threat of my roommate's return prohibited it. By then, I knew the calling card number and PIN by heart and hammered away at the keypad."

Katie nodded and chuckled.

"As the phone began ringing, I wondered if he'd be home. Had he decided to expand the distance between himself and St. Jerry's? I was about to find out. A soft-spoken woman with a high voice answered, and I told her I needed to speak with David.

"She pulled the rug out from under me when she asked, 'Why is that?'

"I told her I was a friend of his, and I hoped to return some of his things. Fearing she'd keep digging for details, I scrambled to develop a more compelling list. Suddenly it occurred to me, I should try to put her on the defensive. So I asked why David took off. I don't know if that was why, but she said she'd get him. While waiting for him, I rehearsed my speech. Just the same, I wasn't ready for our brief exchange.

"When he came to the phone, I told him the guys missed him and asked when he'd be back. All he said was, 'Don't know.'

"At a loss for any other small talk, I told him he left some stuff behind, and I could bring it to him on Friday afternoon.

"He asked, 'What about your classes and practice?' And I told him I had to be up near Bemidji and could drop the stuff off.

"He shot me down when he told me to just keep 'whatever.'

"This is where I pulled out all the stops and lied through my teeth, hoping to set the hook and reel him in. I said I had a 3½-inch computer disk I knew didn't belong to Bud. He wanted to know how I knew it wasn't Bud's.

"For the first time, he showed some interest in what I was saying. I hoped to remain nebulous. If he wanted details, I didn't think I could pull it off. Thankfully, without waiting for an answer, he asked for a detail, but not the type I feared. He wanted to know where it was found.

"I told him it was in his room. Notice I was sensitive enough not to say his and Bud's room.

"He told me to mail it, and I obtained his address— but not because I was going to mail anything.

"I said, 'On second thought, I think I should hang onto it, in the event it isn't yours.'

"He said he'd mail it back if it wasn't, and I said I was going to be in the vicinity the day after tomorrow. If it wasn't his, I wanted to find whomever, because they were probably worried about where they lost it.

"When he asked if I'd accessed it, I told him I thought it would be better to find the owner.

"He asked what time on Friday, and I said it would be sometime between 3:00 and 6:00, but I couldn't be more specific than that.

"By all indications, David and Abigail attended the same telephone etiquette classes. David said he'd see me on Friday and hung up. Or was he trying to save my long-distance minutes?" Pete smiled.

Katie laughed and asked, "Is that known as giving the suspect the benefit of the doubt?"

TWENTY-TWO
Another Country Heard From

Pete figured Katie must be relieved when, as he reached this point, Teddy demanded some attention and no doubt nourishment as well.

She nodded when he suggested a break, then sat in the family room, nursing Teddy and conversing with the two of them.

Pete fixed a salad and prepared steaks for grilling. Having grown accustomed to the quiet that enveloped them most of the time, both jumped when the phone rang. Pete looked at the caller ID and smiled.

"Hey, partner," he answered, "are you cursing me for being gone so long, or are you hoping I never return?"

Martin said, "Will it be enough if I tell you, since becoming an investigator, this has been the longest four weeks of my life?" Pete could sense the smile in his voice.

"Sounds like a good deal, if you're afraid of growing old." Pete laughed.

"The penalties dwarf any potential benefits. You're returning on Monday, right? Or do I have to find another job for Michelle, as well as one for Marty, and retire in an effort to preserve my sanity?"

107

"Come on, Martin, it can't be that bad."

"It's not bad, it's just not the same, and the difference is exceedingly painful. You're coming in on Monday, right?"

"Definitely. I've exhausted my leave, but I owe it to you to be honest, Martin. I'm not sure how long I'll stay."

"Pete, what are you talking about? You love the work."

"I do, and I love my son. It's a tough position to be in."

"Like I don't know that? After all, I have two kids. Until now, you've sailed along with Katie as your only commitment. Trust me. The job is still worth it."

"I'll tell you what, Martin. Katie's feeding Teddy. Want to come over and entertain him, while she and I eat dinner?"

Martin liked the idea, and said he was on his way. While there, he also hoped to, if necessary, convince Pete to remain a homicide detective, not put in just enough time to provide the necessary notice of his resignation.

Awaiting Martin's arrival, Pete finished the salad and readied the grill. Then he joined Katie in the family room and told her about their soon-to-arrive visitor.

Katie smiled. She thought spending the evening with Martin would remind Pete how he missed both Martin and their partnership. She knew they found great satisfaction in both the work and in doing it as a team.

While waiting for Martin, Pete sat with Katie and Teddy, enjoying this time with the two people who owned his heart and with whom he hoped to grow old.

When Martin arrived, he kept his jacket on and joined Pete on the frigid deck, while Pete grilled the steaks. His mouth watered as he thought about how much he liked red meat, as well as his wife's ongoing efforts to minimize his consumption. Taking several steps forward, he bent closer to the grill.

Smell is supposed to be something like 90 percent of taste, right? he thought and tried to take advantage of the possibility. After several deep whiffs, he concluded the other 10 percent was what really mattered.

"Cold?" Pete asked, misinterpreting Martin's move closer to the grill.

"Naw, just checking the marbling on the steaks. They look perfect."

Remembering Martin's love for red meat, and confident he was fibbing, Pete thought, *Bad timing,* and he wished they weren't having steak tonight. "Want to join us, Martin?" he asked. "We have plenty."

"Thanks, I ate just before I came. I could eat one bite, but I'd never be satisfied." *Ahh for the good old days,* he thought, then forced himself to concentrate on how much better he now looked and felt.

Minutes before the steaks were ready, Katie finished nursing Teddy.

Martin joined them at the dining room table and held Teddy while they ate. "I'd almost forgotten how nice this feels," he said, smiling down at Teddy. "You know he looks just like you, don't you, Pete? He could definitely pass as a clone. Is he?" He looked at Katie.

"I'll only answer if you promise it goes no further than this room." Katie chuckled.

When Teddy started crying, Pete pushed back his chair to go get him. It wasn't necessary. Martin put Teddy up against his shoulder and began rubbing his back.

Teddy responded in the way Martin thought and hoped he would. He quieted down.

Pete pulled his chair back up to the table and said, "Dare I ask what's happening at work?"

"Your substitute and I wrapped up a case yesterday. It's now up to the county attorney. Should be a slam dunk. The assistant county attorney is pleased with the case we built."

Tilting his head and looking at Pete out of the corner of his eye, Martin added, "But, it isn't the same without you, Pete."

After Katie took Teddy and headed for the nursery, Martin pulled up close to the table and clasped his hands on top. He spent the rest of his visit delivering the best sales pitch of the dozens he'd concocted, hoping it would succeed and fearing it wouldn't.

Among the points he stressed were that a kid can sense if a parent is happy and content, as well as frustrated, bored, discouraged, discontented, and unhappy. "You love being a homicide detective. How long will you be happy doing something less rewarding and fulfilling? More, as in more time with Teddy, isn't necessarily better, especially when the quality of that time is diminished by a diminished level of happiness."

"And you know, he concluded, we could limit ourselves to eight- or ten-hour days—most of the time. We could even work around a break in the middle of the day."

Pete listened quietly throughout the recitation and nodded from time to time.

After thanking Martin for his efforts and his concern, Pete walked him to the door and said, "See you on Monday. It'll take some time for me to work my way through this. I appreciate your input. It means a lot. Just so you know, if I stay, you'll be a major reason."

Martin punched him in the shoulder, turned, and walked to his car ... without looking back.

TWENTY-THREE
Taking Stock

As soon as Teddy was asleep in his crib, Katie said, "Okay, back to work. I think you still have a few pages to share."

"More like quite a few chapters," Pete said. "Want to take a break until tomorrow?"

"Not a chance."

"Okay, but should I switch to the condensed version? In that case, I could finish in another fifteen or thirty minutes."

"Nope. I want the whole story. This might be the only chance I have to experience an investigation with you. Besides, if this was the trigger that led to you becoming a police officer, reliving it might help you decide what you want to do now."

"A glutton for punishment, huh?" Pete smiled, stretched, and settled back into his dining room chair.

"When I left off," he began, "I'd scheduled meetings with the Bellinghams and David. Before I went to bed that night, I was determined to complete one other, especially important thing. I had to talk to Val's brother Keith. Since I was leaving town the day after the next one, I wanted to make sure I wasn't wasting both time and gas by overlooking someone right under my nose.

"It may seem thus far that I'd ignored him. Not true. After getting his dorm and room number from Val, I'd repeatedly stopped by. Since I never saw him in The Commons, I even bit the bullet and ate at The Refectory a couple of times, hoping to run into him there. Thus far, I'd struck out in both locations. So despite some assignments I should have been concentrating on, I walked over to his dorm, determined to hang around outside his room until he showed up.

"It was a test of both endurance and commitment. Despite asking several guys if they knew where I could find him and learning nothing helpful, I hung out there for almost two hours. Of course, I took a textbook along and completed an assignment in the process.

"Keith looked shocked when he saw me sitting on the floor outside his room, legs stretched out, reading. He asked if my roommate got sick of my crap and kicked me out, then laughed heartily.

"He rolled his eyes when I said my roommate cried when I said I had to be gone for the evening. I told him I was in a hurry to get back before Scott had to check into the infirmary.

"He wanted to know what I ate for dinner 'to be that full of it.'

"With the preliminaries out of the way, I told him I needed ten or fifteen minutes of his time.

"He nodded and invited me into his room.

"Scrutinizing his facial expression, I started by mentioning that Val said Bud helped him with his computer. He nodded then shook his head—I read his expression as sadness ... or maybe regret.

"At a loss for how to proceed, I said, 'He was afraid of you, you know.' Again I watched for his reaction.

"He looked at me questioningly, then asked if I was referring to the day he saw Bud in the bookstore. He went on to explain how guilty he felt about the look he'd given Bud, after he heard Bud died the next day. Said he actually wondered if he'd helped to spoil his last night on earth. He insisted he'd been jerking Bud around and would never have said or done anything to him. He looked sorry.

"I asked, 'You weren't angry about what he had to be planning? Why not?' I was hoping to nudge him toward the truth, if he was handing me a line.

"He said he didn't want Val to stick her nose in his relationships, so he thought he owed her the same consideration. Then he put a hand on my shoulder and asked what decade I was living in.

"I returned to my room convinced he was either innocent or a talented liar. And again that night, I spent more time thinking, evaluating, and second-guessing myself than sleeping. I had trouble abandoning the desire to know what kind of counseling Bud sought from Father Joe. With Win's revelation about the condoms, I couldn't help but wonder if he wanted to get the more liberal wing of the Catholic church's current read on premarital sex. That wouldn't have surprised me.

"Then there was Mr. Bellingham's death. The timing seemed too coincidental. And what about David? The screen saver on Bud's monitor should have been on when David arrived in their room. In that case, David wouldn't have seen the 'suicide' note, unless he'd fiddled with Bud's computer. If he did, why? Did he type that note? Or was Bud right? Was David stealing stuff off his computer? Why did David immediately take off for home? Was he so freaked over Bud's death that he had to get away? Or was it something else? My questions multiplied ... How about Kennedy Lansing? Did he know Bud was Val's current boyfriend? Was he so attached to Val that he had to get rid of any competition? How, in the course of a few weeks, could he become familiar enough with Bud's schedule and habits to pull it off? The current list of suspects was far from complete. So far, I'd barely scratched the surface. Knowing my approach could make or break my investigation, I thought long and hard about how to handle the questioning. I worked to make it a conversation, not an interrogation.

"Early on, I'd realized my ability to get anyone under consideration to talk would improve if they thought I believed Bud killed himself. That way, I wouldn't force anyone who believed that to defend their position. I'd also avoid putting the murderer on the defensive or motivate them to refuse to talk to me. So I began conversations with those under consideration by telling them I was still trying to cope with Bud's suicide. Then I talked about how hard it was to get to know Bud and asked if they succeeded in getting past his armor. Followed with questions I hoped would get them to talk about him. Sometimes it worked. Sometimes it fell flat. Bud was a loner, and that complicated things.

"Regardless of how they answered those questions, I said Bud sometimes got under my skin and watched carefully for a reaction. I wasn't crazy or optimistic enough to think that would result in a confession. I did think whoever did it might be happy to hear he wasn't the only one, and a brief flash of relief might cross his face.

Pete paused, then said, "I keep saying 'he,' Katie. Whereas I hadn't totally discounted the possibility his killer was a woman, I was 99 percent sure it wasn't. Thus far, I'd spoken with almost half of the students in Bud's chem lab and had mixed emotions about what I'd achieved in the process. Could all those people be so unfamiliar with a fellow student? All they seemed to know about him was what they assumed, based on the frequency and quality of his responses to the questions posed by Dr. Newport. I hadn't spoken with his lab partner yet, but still ...

"I created a checklist to track everyone with whom I spoke. I was able to check off the names of more than half of the students on his dorm floor and all the students on my dorm floor. By the way, not a single person disagreed with my declared conclusion that Bud committed suicide.

"I had yet to meet with Bud's philosophy professor. As with the chem lab proctor, I wanted to get Professor Odessa's take on Bud in general, Bud's demeanor in his last class on the last day of his life, and obtain a class roster. I hoped to succeed Wednesday, on my third attempt.

Pete stretched out his arms and legs and said, "Let me back up a minute, Katie. I could have emailed this professor on Monday or Tuesday and tried to set up a meeting. The thing was, crazy as it may sound, I thought I'd get better cooperation if I saw him in person. I thought that way I could either explain what I was doing or skirt the issue, if it felt like that would serve me better. Can't do that with an email. If my efforts at finding him didn't succeed on Wednesday, I'd resort to email."

TWENTY-FOUR
Professor Odessa

"Reaching his classroom in time to find Professor Odessa collecting the books, notebooks, and handouts that littered the desk in the front of the room, I broke into a broad smile. He smiled back at me. I had no idea if he knew who I was or was simply being friendly.

"Waving me in, he motioned me over to one of the desks, then sat next to me and said, 'Rumor has it you've been trying to corner me.'

"I must have looked puzzled, because he said, 'Richmond.'

"Turned out, their paths had crossed, and Dr. Richmond asked if he'd met with me. He'd hung around longer than normal that day, just in case. *Thank goodness for Dr. Richmond*, I thought, then thanked Professor Odessa for his thoughtfulness.

"He asked what was so 'all fired important,' and I said Sterling Callaway was a good friend, and I was searching for answers, regarding his death.

"'Does the word suicide leave a bad taste in your mouth?,' he asked. Without pulling any punches, I said, 'Definitely when it's a misnomer.'

117

"He nodded, and I jumped right in with my first question, asking if he thought Bud seemed depressed in the days leading up to his last day on earth. He shook his head and said 'No,' and added, 'and that's what I told the police.' He knew his class was the last one Bud ever attended, and it ended about an hour before he died.

"I asked if he was aware of anything different about Bud that day or in the preceding days, or anything that might have been particularly upsetting to him. This time, before answering, he stopped to consider the question. Then he blew out a long, slow breath and said something happened about a week earlier.

"Since he left it at that, I asked if he was willing to share the details. He shook his head and said it was still under investigation. All he'd tell me was that originally he'd suspected Bud of something, confronted him, and discovered it couldn't be him.

"Utilizing what Kyle said about catching David on Bud's computer, and what Win said about Bud's journal, I asked if Bud's computer or computer expertise played a part in it. He gave me a sidelong glance and asked if I got that information from Bud.

"Becoming as uncommunicative as the professor, I said, 'I hadn't heard anything until *after* Bud died.'

"Since he told me Bud didn't seem depressed the last days of his life, I asked him to describe Bud's emotional state at the time.

"He said Bud's last day was particularly memorable, and not only because it was the last time he saw him. It was because 'Bud seemed so happy, so lighthearted, content.'

"'In love?' I asked.

"'That would certainly explain it.' He nodded. His eyes, but not his mouth, smiled.

"When I asked about Bud's interactions with his fellow students, he said they were largely nonexistent. He was of the same opinion as Dr. Newport. Most of Bud's talking consisted of answering questions in class.

"'Early on,' he said, 'some students contended he had an unfair advantage and didn't belong in that class. They claimed it was obvious he'd previously covered the class materials.'

"Odessa said he didn't make any points with them when he said they wouldn't feel so inadequate if they read the assignments *before* class, rather than waiting until the night before a test.

"Bud's performance irritated those who believed he was skewing the curve, but the animosity seemed to diminish greatly after Odessa assured the class that a single student could not throw off the entire curve on which they were graded. Worst case, he told them, that person or grade would be treated as an outlier.

"He was amazed at the number of puzzled looks that sparked, but he didn't translate the statement for them. He figured anyone who at this point didn't know the meaning should look it up.

"I asked if he ever saw Bud walking toward or along the trail that ran along the bluffs, and he said he spotted him walking in that direction occasionally, on Fridays, when he left early to go to his son's baseball games. He added, 'I take Garrett to some St. Jerome's games, Pete. You're one of his favorite players. He told me you should be playing second. Says they're wasting your talents by keeping you at third.'

"Yeah, Katie, I smiled, but the comment didn't deter me. I repeated that question, and he said he hadn't seen Bud walking in that direction that fateful Wednesday. Incidentally, this meeting occurred exactly four weeks after Bud died. So I asked if he ever saw anyone else heading for that path. Of course, what I was interested in was that particular Wednesday, but anything else might also be helpful.

"He said he occasionally saw people going there, but couldn't identify any of them and hadn't observed any regulars. He believed the traffic was much heavier when some of the guys took their girls there—'in search of privacy.'

"Unfortunately, he didn't see anyone going that way the day Bud was murdered.

"Again, I got a list of the students who had been in Bud's class. Here's another particularly interesting detail. David was, or at least had been, in this class. That had me wondering if this was the class in which Bud thought David might be cheating. It would explain Odessa's refusal to provide any details about the Bud-related incident."

TWENTY-FIVE
Bud's Family, The Callaways

"Thursday and Friday were jam packed, so I planned to spend every available minute on Wednesday, eliminating as many people as possible from further consideration. That's what I planned. What I accomplished was another story. Trust me, Katie, you don't want to hear that one. It was a tale of frustration and disappointment. By the time I hung it up for the day, I'd done nothing noteworthy. For that reason, I'll jump ahead to Thursday afternoon.

"I skipped both of my afternoon classes. Had no choice when it came to the second, and I thought the professor for the first would prefer I skip it, rather than cut out early. I used that time to load my backpack with the three sets of driving directions, a change of clothes, toiletries, a baseball cap, sunglasses, a couple of notebooks, and a handful of pens and pencils.

"Then, in an effort to keep us hydrated, I hustled over to The Commons and bought a large Coke for me and a large Diet Coke for Andrea. Arrived back at my dorm with about fifteen minutes to spare, but stayed put. I was anxious to hit the road as soon as she arrived.

"She arrived ten minutes early, jumped out of the car, kissed me, and asked, 'Ready to solve this thing?'

"I appreciated the positive attitude. She offered to let me drive, and I said I was happy riding or driving. So she took the first shift.

"Before starting out, I pulled the directions to Madison out of my backpack and looked at the fuel gauge. The tank was full. At a few minutes to three, we were on our way.

"In the back seat, Andrea had a large bag filled with chips, cookies, candy bars, nuts, and granola bars. She also stocked the console with the same and told me to help myself. I spent the first couple of hours absorbed in updating her on my efforts, telling her about the arrangements I'd made, and outlining our preliminary schedule. She was happy to hear we'd have time to pull into a rest stop rather than driving through the night.

"I told her about my call to the Bellinghams and that I hoped she might be able to speak with Murray, since it seemed unlikely he'd talk to me.

"When she smiled and asked if I was paying by the word, I said only if three of the words were, 'I did it.'

"I was thankful for Andrea's companionship. The trip was pleasant but long. With the majority of the miles via freeways, it didn't offer much in the way of scenery. I could have spent the time singing along with the radio, but ... as much as I like to sing, in six hours I might have had to tell myself to stow it." Pete rolled his eyes.

"We reached the Callaways' a little after 7:00. Andrea drove the whole way, and her right foot is a touch heavy. Don't get me wrong, Katie, I'm not complaining." Pete grinned.

Katie laughed and said, "I didn't think so. If you had a problem with your driver exceeding the speed limit,

you and Martin would be incompatible. Besides, I'm
confident you have nothing against arriving early."

"The Callaways lived in a white two-story traditional-
style home in an upper-middle-class neighborhood. I
introduced Andrea to Win and his parents. They insisted
there was sufficient time, and we had to eat something.

"Too nervous and distracted to think about food, the
only thing I'd eaten on the way was a granola bar, and
Andrea had eaten little more. So we didn't argue.

"While Mrs. Callaway made a salad and heated
leftover wild rice and hamburger hotdish, Win and his
dad took us to Bud's bedroom to get his sash and the
medallion.

"I was surprised how hard being in his room hit me.
Everything about it was so Bud. He had a huge Lego
reproduction of the Apollo 11 command module, and
one of the Columbia and its lunar module, the Eagle.
This was before Lego began releasing the large kits, so
he must have designed them himself. Stacked along the
walls stood all kinds of storage containers filled with
hundreds of Lego pieces. The only thing hanging on the
walls was a poster of the International Space Station.
Because NASA is so computer-dependent, none of that
surprised me.

"My eyes grew moist, but I did my best to conceal
that from Bud's dad and brother, as I carefully tucked
the sash and medallion into my backpack. Don't know if
I succeeded. Neither they nor Andrea mentioned it, but
at least with Andrea, that wasn't a valid indicator.

"All three Callaways sat with us while we ate. The hot
dish was amazing. In fact, I asked for the recipe. Gave
both Mom and Grandma Jackie a copy. We ate quickly,
not because we were short on time, but because I was
anxious to get some answers from the Bellinghams.

"While we ate, Bud's dad talked about his business. He was a political consultant, and it was interesting to hear what that entailed, including the level of commitment required, the number of people he had to schmooze, and how often he had to negotiate compromises between people with the same proclaimed goals. By the time he'd finished, I knew I wanted nothing to do with a career like that.

"Win told us all about the 1973 Monte Carlo he was getting back in tip-top shape. It had been up on blocks for years. Whereas he was in college studying business, like Bud told me, cars were his passion ... in addition to girls. Win didn't say anything about the latter." Pete chuckled.

"Bud's mom said little, other than to thank us profusely for coming and for all we were doing to figure out what happened to Bud. Her eyes were tear-filled when I hugged her good-bye.

"They walked us out to the car and wished us godspeed. They didn't ask to be notified of the outcome of our next stop. Guess they knew I'd let them know if we learned anything noteworthy."

TWENTY-SIX
The Bellinghams

"The sun set before we left the Callaways, but as we drove away, there was still sufficient light to illuminate the details of the structures and vegetation we passed en route to the Bellinghams. That changed, however, before we arrived.

"On the way, Andrea and I discussed what we needed to achieve while with them. She wanted to know if I thought it was likely that any or all of them had killed Bud. We talked about ways we hoped to either prove they had or remove them from consideration. Both would be difficult at best. We had nothing to go on, no one pointing the finger at them, no sign that any of them had traveled to Minnesota.

"I hoped to get Abigail talking and see where it led. I also tried to remain optimistic that Murray would talk to Andrea, in hopes that would lead somewhere. As I mentioned earlier, due to the purported suicide of their dad, I didn't really want any of them, with the possible exception of their dad, to be guilty. Couldn't help wondering if murdering Bud weighed so heavily on him that he'd killed himself.

"The clock had yet to strike 8:30 as Andrea parked in front of the Bellingham home. She smiled and touched a finger to her lips, then touched it to my cheek. 'Here's hoping whatever you're wishing for happens,' she said and reached for the door handle.

"The fact it was pitch dark by the time we arrived was both beneficial and detrimental. It was harder to read the house numbers and see the environs clearly, but indoor lights might show when someone was home.

"The Bellinghams lived on a cul de sac in a ranch-style house. Approaching the front door, I scanned their home as best I could, wondering what if anything it revealed about the family.

"A guy in dire need of a diet and an exercise regime answered the door and said, 'If it was up to me, you wouldn't cross the threshold.' As he completed that proclamation, a petite woman who appeared to be our age came up behind him, called him Murray, and told him to step aside and let us in.

"Trying to endear herself to Murray, Andrea piped right up and said she was sorry to hear about the loss of their dad and to be bothering them at a time like this. She added that Murray had every right to be angry with us. Then she asked if he'd keep her company while his sister spoke with me. He shrugged and waved us in.

"Andrea followed him into the living room, and Abigail moved in that direction. I redirected Abigail's path when I asked if we might find a place where our conversation wouldn't interfere with Murray and Andrea's and vice versa.

"She nodded and led me through the foyer, past the kitchen and laundry room to the family room. On the way, she looked back over her shoulder and asked if I'd like something to drink.

"I declined her offer.

"The family room was large with comfortable furniture arranged around a massive entertainment center that included bookshelves holding a set of encyclopedias. Abigail settled in a recliner, so I took the matching one. After taking a deep breath and saying a quick prayer, I began by reiterating Andrea's condolences. Abigail's only response was a nod.

"On the way to Madison, Andrea and I spent a chunk of time trying to concoct a leadoff question that would get Abigail talking, without mentioning Bud. The challenge was getting her to bring him up and see what she said.

"Knowing that, at best, I was taking the long way around, I asked her where she was going to school. Then I asked how she liked it, if she had any ideas about the field of study she'd pursue, et cetera.

"After a few minutes of this, she smiled and said she knew I wasn't in the process of compiling her biography, so why was I there?

"Sweat trickled down my back as I attempted to explain, innocuously, that I was there about Sterling Callaway.

"She said she'd heard the news and felt bad for his family—especially his parents. 'No parent should have to bury their son or daughter.'

"I asked how she'd learned about his death, and she said several of their fellow students had called.

"I told her that rumor had it there was no love lost between them and, without looking away, she said she assumed I was talking about the valedictorian award for their class. She said she liked Bud, and he deserved the award. Said she was furious with her dad and Murray when they tried to, as she put it, 'steal it from him through all kinds of shenanigans.' Then she added, 'It's all a matter of mathematics, and Bud had earned it.' Math was never her dad's or her brother's strong suit, she said with a frown.

"'To them, it was strictly a matter of loyalty?' I asked, and she said that was both 'kind and accurate.' She said she valued loyalty, 'but not when it's taken to extremes and hurts others in the process.'

"'Who did it hurt?' I asked, hoping she had something to reveal ... and would.

"All she mentioned was how nasty they were to Bud on graduation day.

"I sat there, trying to be clever, trying to come up with a question that would cause her to spill her guts. That, of course, was indicative of my vocabulary in those days, Katie. Now I'd say something far more refined, such as 'divulge all of the relevant and damaging details.'" Pete smiled.

"Of course you would, Pete. I often refer to you as the sesquipedalian who stole my heart."

Katie laughed, and Pete crossed his eyes.

"Okay, back to my tale of mystery and intrigue. Abby, by then she'd asked me to refer to her that way, shrugged when I asked if Murray still hated Bud.

"When asked if she and Bud had been friends, she blushed and said she had a crush on him freshman and sophomore years, but they were never really friends.

"'Then?' I asked.

"She said she gave up and started dating another guy, so she didn't have to sit home every Friday and Saturday night. They dated their junior and senior years, and she hadn't seen or heard from him since. He went to Villanova. At Madison, she met a nice guy, and they'd been dating for almost six months.

"When asked if she'd known where Bud went to college, she said she only knew it was somewhere in Minnesota. She then asked if I was from Minnesota.

"I nodded and, before she could say anything else, I asked if she and her family had ever been to Minnesota.

"Abby hadn't been there, but her dad and brother had. She said a short time before he died, her dad took Murray to see North Dakota State University in Fargo, Bemidji State University, and the University of Minnesota Morris. That revelation elicited a stream of tears, and she left me long enough to find and return with a box of tissues.

"After sitting back down and collecting herself, she finished the thought, telling me Murray wanted something small. He balked at anything the size of the University of Wisconsin in Madison or Milwaukee. Also, his grades hadn't gotten him any scholarships, so 'he had to look for something on the lower end of the tuition scale.'

"Much as I hated to stay on that topic, I asked if they went on a weekend, so Murray didn't have to miss school.

"She said as much as her dad wanted to do it that way, none of the schools they wanted to visit offered tours and meetings with professors on weekends.

"By then, of course, a cacophony of alarms and whistles was sounding in my head. After taking a deep breath, I asked if she remembered the dates of those visits.

"Through sobs, she said all she knew was it was the Tuesday, Wednesday, and Thursday two weeks before her dad died. That placed them in North Dakota or Minnesota the day Bud died! So I was anxious to narrow it down, but out of deference to Abby, I asked if she could handle a few more questions about that.

"She bit her lip and nodded, so I asked if they'd moved from west to east to reduce the drive time home.

"She didn't know.

"I asked, 'Since they were in the vicinity, did they take the time to check in with Bud and look at St. Jerome's?'

"She said she had no idea where Bud was going to school and doubted they did. Also, she didn't think there was any way the tuition at St. Jerome's would have been 'doable' for her family.

"That had me wondering if Murray would now be able to go to college. I also wondered if scholarships would carry Abby through the drop in family income that may have resulted from her dad's death. I liked her, and I hoped so.

"I didn't think Abby was withholding information, but decided to check whether increasing her sympathy for Bud's family might uncover additional details. So I said the police told the Callaways they were looking at suicide as a possibility in Bud's death.

"When I said that, Abby gasped and covered her face. I continued, unchecked by her reaction, and told her the whole family was distraught and having trouble coping. Said I was worried about their ability to move on if that was true.

"She said she hoped and prayed the police determined it wasn't suicide and found whoever killed Bud. She said he was a wonderful person, and he would have gone far. By the time she'd finished, she was sobbing, and I felt guilty for using suicide as a weapon.

"It didn't seem or feel like I had anything additional to gain from this meeting, so I thanked her for speaking with me. I also said I'd say a prayer for her and her family. I meant it.

"She stood, and we went in search of Andrea and Murray. Andrea jumped to her feet when she saw me.

"Murray stood and lumbered over to Abigail and me.

"I knew from her expression that Andrea hadn't gotten anywhere, but forced myself to remain optimistic. Before we left, I tried one last approach with Murray. Carefully watching his expression, I said I heard he'd been in Minnesota, looking at colleges. He didn't react. So I said the viewpoint of another student is often far more valuable than the sales pitch the school offers. Andrea agreed to show him around St. Cloud State, and I told him I had a friend in Bemidji—'if he's interested.'

"He stood there, gawking at me, appearing surprised at the offer, but he didn't look like I'd just revealed that I knew 'the truth, the whole truth, and nothing but the truth.' He just shrugged wordlessly.

"Again, Abby took charge, dismissing us by reaching for the doorknob and wishing us safe travels."

TWENTY-SEVEN
Back to the Callaways

"I sure missed Bud, and thus far the joy I experienced while standing in his room and eating dinner at the Callaways' were the highlights of my trip.

"Since I hadn't had to offer the sash or medallion to Murray or Abigail, I still had both in my backpack. Because I didn't want to risk anything happening to them, I asked Andrea if she was okay with dropping them off at the Callaways' before heading to Bemidji.

"She thought it was a good idea, and it wasn't far out of the way. So we retraced our steps, hoping to find lights on in their home. It seemed likely, since it was only 9:30, and Win struck me as a night owl.

"Had we passed a pay phone on the way, I would have called, but that didn't happen. Thankfully, the house was well lit as Andrea pulled up to the curb.

"Win looked shocked to see us standing at their door. Said right after we left, his mom realized they should have invited us to spend the night. She wondered where we'd stay, and worried we might plan to drive through the night. Since this was prior to cellphones, their only way to reach us was to call the Bellinghams, and they didn't dare do that.

"That's when Bud's mom joined us, wearing a broad smile. 'Telepathy?' she asked.

"I opened my backpack, removed the sash and medallion, and said, 'Or the chance to return these to you.'

"She started crying when I handed her the bundle and asked if we were returning both.

"I said we hadn't needed either, and she grabbed me and gave me a long, warm hug.

"She begged us to stay. Said I could stay in Bud's room, and Andrea could stay in the guest room. Both would be ready in a couple of minutes.

"It occurred to me she might prefer that Bud was the last one to stay in his room, so I said I'd like to sleep in the living room on the couch. I told her a sheet and a pillow were all I needed. Can't guarantee it, Katie, but I'll always believe I saw a look of relief cross her face."

Katie nodded.

"It was a good choice. We hadn't yet been in their warm and inviting living room. The back wall was all windows. On the left was a fireplace surrounded by built-in bookshelves. They held pictures of the whole family, including Bud, Win, and their sister as babies, small children, preteens, and teenagers. Thankful for the opportunity and missing Bud, I studied them before I turned in for the night.

"In front of the windows stood a sofa long enough for me to stretch out on, and I knew I'd be more comfortable there than in Bud's room for that reason as well.

"The next morning, when the sun was shining, I looked through the wall of windows. Discovered the Callaway home backed up to a park filled with huge deciduous trees and evergreens, walking paths, a baseball diamond, and basketball hoops. This had to be a great house for raising kids. We'd spent the night in far more comfort than any rest stop would have provided. Got up at 7:00 Friday morning. Enjoyed a delicious breakfast of eggs, sausage, and homemade blueberry muffins.

"None of the Callaways said a word about our meetings with the Bellinghams, and I admired their restraint. I broached the subject as Andrea and I finished breakfast. I told them we'd obtained some interesting and possibly key details and I wouldn't know if the Bellinghams were involved until I got some answers—if it was even possible to obtain a timeline, regarding Murray and his dad's college visits.

"I admitted my gut reaction was none of them had done it and, in light of Mr. Bellingham's suicide, found myself hoping they hadn't.

"Bud's mom said the word amongst her friends was he hadn't committed suicide. They said he was in a serious car accident just before Christmas and had been pain-ridden ever since. His doctors refused to prescribe a strong enough dose of oxycodone, so in an effort to control the pain, he took multiple pills at a time and took them more often than prescribed. They heard that's what killed him.

"Hearing that, I hoped none of the Bellinghams were guilty. Even so, I couldn't drop them from the list of suspects until I had proof of their innocence. Then I asked something I'd wanted to ask Abby, but hadn't had the heart. 'What did Mr. Bellingham do for a living?'

"It turned out he taught auto body and car repair in a vo-tech. That had to be all but impossible for someone in constant pain, and I felt even worse for wishing he'd been the one I was after."

TWENTY-EIGHT
Bemidji or Bust

"We were on the road by 8:00 that morning. Might have been on our way a bit earlier, but it took quite some time for the Callaways to thank us in a way they considered adequate.

"Andrea didn't say a word about who would drive. She just got behind the wheel again. So in my trademark 'easy-going manner,' I remained the copilot and head map reader."

Pete paused and asked, "Do you think that was a prediction of what lay ahead, when Martin and I became partners, Katie?"

Katie chuckled and said, "Sounds like it was your destiny, Pete."

"I retrieved the printout of the route MapQuest recommended from Madison to Bemidji. With Andrea behind the wheel, I figured we'd make the seven-and-a-half-hour trip in a little under seven hours. So we should arrive in Bemidji at around 3:00, all things being equal. However, again they were not.

"While traveling north on Highway 64, we passed through the Paul Bunyan State Forest. That was the first time I'd heard of it, and I marveled at the size of the trees. Aspen appeared to dominate the landscape, and there was a smattering of pines, including a lot of magnificent jack pines. I thoroughly enjoyed staring in awe during this part of the trip.

"Not long after leaving the park, I saw a sign saying we were six miles from Laporte and twenty-eight miles from Bemidji. I should have asked Andrea to check the odometer when I saw it, because a minute later it happened. We were making great time and less than thirty minutes from our destination when the car started making a *clunk, clunk, clunk* or a *thump, thump, thump* sound.

"I looked questioningly at Andrea, and she said, 'Flat tire.'

"*No big deal*, I thought. *I can change a tire.*

"Andrea opened the trunk, and we looked at each other in disbelief. There was no spare tire.

"Based on the sign I saw about a mile before, LaPorte was roughly five miles ahead of us, and only the town-free park lay behind us. If I knew the odometer reading when we passed that sign, I could have estimated the distance to Laporte more accurately. But I didn't so … Today, the distance wouldn't be a big deal. We could call for help. But Andrea didn't own a cellphone either.

"We'd passed few cars going in either direction on that road, and not a one had passed us.

"I asked if she'd be okay staying with the car while I walked to the next town, and she nodded. Today, Katie, based on what I've seen in my years as a police officer, I'd never have left her there alone.

"I didn't walk. I ran. Figured I could run the estimated distance in a half hour or less, and I was grateful it was a cool, spring day. After ten or twelve minutes, I must have looked desperate or the fact I was in the middle of nowhere alarmed the first driver I saw. Traveling in the opposite direction, an elderly man with a thick mane of snow-white hair pulled over, rolled down his window, and asked if I needed help.

"Panting, I told him I had a flat tire and no spare, that I needed to get a spare and get it back to the car.

"He asked where the car was, and I thrust my thumb back over my shoulder and said it was 'three or four miles back that way.'

"He said to get in, and he'd help me find a tire and get it back to the car.

"I knew Andrea would be nervously counting the minutes, so I told him my girlfriend was with the car and asked if he'd mind going and telling her before we did so. We did, and thankfully he knew enough to check inside the driver's side door for the tire size *before* we went in search of a tire.

"Anyway, I was glad Dad had insisted I have a credit card for emergencies. I bought the new tire with that card, installed it, secured the flat in the trunk, and we headed out while our guardian angel waved good-bye.

"We reached Bemidji at 4:00, happy to have made it in one piece ... plus a spare. By the way, back then you could replace a flat tire. Today, you might have to replace all four tires. My credit limit wouldn't have covered four tires." Pete shook his head.

"Thank goodness you're so old." Katie smiled.

"As we reached the city limits, I thought about calling David to say we were on our way. Then decided it might be a mistake, in the event ... I hoped the tire business wasn't a sign of what lay ahead.

"The Elmores lived in a well-kept, brick, one-story, ranch-style house.

"Andrea smiled and said, 'We made it, quite a bit worse for the wear.' Then we both took a deep breath and hiked to the front door of a house that was set back off the road on a sizable lot.

"David took his sweet time in answering the doorbell, and that did nothing to help my anxiety level. I didn't know what to think when I saw him. He looked like he hadn't slept in days ... or weeks.

"I held out a hand and said it was good to see him. It was, but not because I'd missed him. Quite honestly, however, I had been worried about him after he took off the way he did.

"David's grip was limp, and his hand felt moist and cool. He said it was nice seeing me but appeared totally unenthused about it. After standing there for several seconds, he seemed to wake up and asked us in.

"Stepping inside the door, the first thing I noticed was the smell of chocolate chip cookies. My mouth began watering.

"'Is this okay?' David asked, signaling the living room. The house had an open floorplan, and I was looking for something isolated. So I asked if there were more private options. He said we could meet in the office down the hall and pointed in that direction. That would be fine, but I wondered what to do about Andrea.

"His sister must have had extrasensory perception, because that's when she appeared and introduced herself. There was a strong family resemblance. Both David and Lily were tall and slender. David was on the verge of six feet and Lily about five nine. Both had wavy, light-brown hair, large blue eyes, arched eyebrows, and full lips.

"David wore a misshapen T-shirt and blue jeans with one of the knees torn out. It looked like he hadn't showered, shaved, or combed his hair. Lily, on the other hand, looked like she didn't have a single hair out of place."

"Wait a minute," Katie said. "You haven't yet described how Andrea looked back then."

"Are you sure?" Pete asked, stroking the skin between his nose and upper lip.

"I'm positive. I'm paying close attention. Haven't missed a single word, and I'd remember."

"Well, if you're sure, she was six foot six and a real bruiser. That's why I always felt safe when I was with her." Pete grinned.

"Come on, Pete."

While recounting the story, he'd spent much of the time looking through and past Katie, focusing on the past that was half a lifetime away. Now he looked at her and answered her question. "Andrea was an inch or so shorter and a pound or two heavier than you. She wore her blonde hair long and had blue eyes. She stole my heart, and I was confident that we'd grow old together. After the car accident destroyed that dream, I was sure I'd never again feel that way about anyone. I'm so glad you came along and proved me wrong, Katie."

He concluded by smiling and reaching across the table to squeeze her hand. Then he continued the story, "Perhaps in an attempt to fill the uncomfortable silence, Lily mentioned she'd been fixing dinner. Aware of my desire for a private meeting with David, Andrea asked if there was any way she could help. Lily said 'Sure,' and that solved my first problem.

"On their way to the kitchen, Lily turned back and asked if she could get me anything.

"I told her anything at all to drink would be wonderful, hoping she'd toss in a few cookies for good measure.

"The compact office where David led me had a desk with a computer and monitor, a desk chair, bookshelves, a comfortable upholstered chair, and a large window. David sat in the desk chair, then motioned me toward the other chair, which sat in front of the window.

"I opened with a question I hoped would put him on the defensive. Said I knew Bud better than anyone and asked why he told the police and everyone else that he'd been suicidal.

"He looked at me like I was some kind of idiot and said he did it 'because of the note on Bud's computer.'

"When I asked what indications he had prior to that, he only shrugged. Staying the course, I asked who knew Bud better than me, and he shrugged again, this time warily.

"'How did you happen to notice the message on his computer?' I asked.

"David stared wordlessly into space.

"I continued, 'His screen saver was on when you walked into your room, wasn't it?' And he moved his concentration from the window behind me to his hands.

"'You touched his mouse or his keyboard, and that shut down the screensaver, right?' I persisted, and David shook his head feverishly.

"When I asked when Bud gave him permission to use his computer or access his files, he didn't respond, so I demanded to know what business he had messing around with Bud's computer.

"He sat stone-faced and remained silent.

"That's when I pounced on him and said through clenched teeth, 'You created that message and fabricated the rumor he was suicidal to cover up for murdering him, didn't you, David.' It was a statement, not a question."

TWENTY-NINE
David Elmore

"'I didn't do any of that!' David screamed, and Lily was there with us within a nanosecond.

"David looked at her repentantly and said, 'Sorry, Lily, I overreacted. Everything's fine. Please finish dinner. Mom and Dad will be home soon, and you know how Dad is.'

"Not knowing their dad, I wondered how much he had to do with who David was.

"Unfortunately, David seemed to recover and regain his composure during that brief pause. As soon as we were alone, he held out a hand and asked, 'Where's my disk?'

"When I didn't respond, he added, 'The one you found and assumed is mine. It is. It must be. I went through my stuff and discovered I'm missing one. I need that disk!'

"This time I was the one who shrugged. I said that I lied about the disk, that I hadn't found one.

"He grimaced and shook his head as his face went slack, and his eyes grew moist.

"Unwilling to get sidetracked from my efforts to identify Bud's killer, I tried another angle. I asked, 'What

142

drove you to it, David?' I was reaching. It was a wide-open question, and I hoped he'd misinterpret how much I knew and tell me both what he'd done and why.

"David closed his eyes, clenched his fists, and spilled his guts. He said, 'Everything came so easy to Bud,' and he was the 'shining star in our philosophy class.' After David got his second C-minus, he was terrified he might lose his scholarship, so he did something he never before thought he was capable of nor would stoop to. In the process, he added, he'd contradicted Pierre Teilhard de Chardin—or he was an exception. He was not advancing spiritually.

"He described how one afternoon, about a month into the semester, as soon as Bud left, he found Bud's current philosophy paper on his computer. He said he didn't copy it. He just breezed through it and used the main points to write his paper. 'It worked like a charm.' He got his first A in that class.

"He repeated the process for the next two papers, and that's when Professor Odessa started calling on him in class, even when he hadn't raised his hand. The professor had never done that before and never did it with anyone else. For that reason, he thought Bud might have blown the whistle on him.

"When Bud died, David knew he could never keep up the charade. Professor Odessa assigned a term paper ten days before Bud died. It would count for 50 percent of their grade. It wasn't due for a month, but Bud never waited until the last minute ... or even the last few weeks. So David checked Bud's computer the weekend before he died, hoping to at least find some notes. Nothing. He did the same the day before Bud died and was surprised he hadn't yet started it. He intended to check again that

Wednesday, and that's when he saw the note on the monitor and freaked.

"Shocked and numb from Bud's death, try as he might, he couldn't write a paper that succeeded in interpreting the concepts. He said he was into math, 'the cut and dried,' and his brain just didn't work that way. He wanted to be an engineer, 'not another Aristotle.'

"David knew that submitting another C- paper would erase any remaining doubts the professor had about what had been happening, so he fled for the security of his home. When I called him and said I'd found a disk, he thought Bud might have been working on the paper and saving it to a disk, rather than to the hard drive, and he thought that disk might save him.

"Based on what Win told me was in Bud's journal, I wondered if Bud planned to write a D paper for that assignment, save it on his hard drive, and let David submit it, while he kept the 'real' paper on a floppy disk. I'd never know.

"If a suicidal person tended to look a particular way, I wasn't aware of it. Even so, the way David looked at that moment provided the perfect portrayal of what I'd anticipate. So I felt compelled to reach out to him.

"Convinced that he hadn't killed Bud, I asked David what I could do to help.

"He shook his head and started crying. I told him there had to be something that he, or he and I together, could do, and we needed to figure it out.

"David moaned and said, 'I've thrown it all away.' He said he cheated to keep from losing his scholarship, and now he'd lose it for sure, and he couldn't afford to stay at St. Jerry's without it. Besides, with this on his academic record, he was sure he'd never get accepted by another college. He moaned again, saying, 'I was so stupid!'

"He wore the most forsaken look I'd ever seen, times ten."

THIRTY
Desperation

"**A**fter I offered to help and said I'd call the next day, I gave David my phone number and asked him to think about my offer. Then Andrea and I got in Rick's car for the trip back to St. Jerry's. David and Lily stood on the front steps, watching as we drove away. Lily was clenching David's right arm. This had been a long and exhausting twenty-seven hours.

"On our way to Bemidji, I'd planned to make a side trip to Bemidji State University. Thought I'd speak with the appropriate person and determine if and when Murray and his dad had been there. However, the flat tire eliminated any chance of it happening that day. If we drove to the university that late, by the time we got there, anyone who might have helped us would have hung it up for the day.

"Heading back to St. Jerry's, I contemplated my meeting with David and felt horrible. For the first time, I wondered if I should end my search ... immediately.

"Andrea knew I was stressed, but not why. She spent the trip back to St. Jerry's trying and failing to cheer me up. This was something I needed some alone time to work my way through.

146

"We reached St. Jerry's at 7:00. Andrea called Rick to see if she could delay her return by another hour. Since he was okay with it, we went to town and out to dinner. I wasn't very good company, so we made short shrift of it. As soon as we got back to school, I hugged and kissed her and thanked her for all she'd done for me. I asked her to call me to let me know when she was back safe and sound. Then thinking about the flat tire, I asked if I could ride along to St. Cloud. I told her I could catch a Greyhound back. But she kissed me again, insisted she'd be fine, and drove away."

Pete looked at Katie and said, "Would you prefer that I leave out those kinds of details?"

Katie laughed and said, "No need to spare the gore on my account. I have a strong stomach, and I can handle it."

Pete smiled and continued, "I worried about how many miles were left in the other three tires. For that reason, I didn't rest easy until Andrea called at 8:45 and said she was back at school. I was exhausted from the meeting with David, and the flat tire hadn't helped anything. So I went to bed early ... but couldn't sleep. After an hour, I got up and composed an email to Professor Odessa.

"The subject was 'Urgent!!' I wanted to use a whole string of exclamation points, but thought less might be better. My message thanked him for the time he'd spent answering my questions earlier that week. Then I told him it was critical I meet with him again 'ASAP.' I didn't want to be melodramatic, but I wanted him to take this email seriously and grant my request. So I said I didn't know when he'd see this message, but would appreciate a reply as soon as he did. I also included my phone number. I ended by saying, I feared a life might depend on his and my actions. 'Yes, I was serious; and no, that life wasn't mine.'

"As soon as I sent it, I began watching my inbox, doubting I'd hear from him before Monday, but hoping nonetheless."

THIRTY-ONE
Will He or Won't He?

"**Y**ou aren't going to believe this, Katie. Professor Odessa responded about ten minutes later. I said a prayer after sending the email, and I said another when I saw his response appear in my inbox.

"He started by saying he was surprised to hear from me on a Friday night, and my message raised his curiosity and his concern. He provided his phone number and said I could call him as soon as I saw his response. God was smiling down on me, because Scott was off somewhere. So I grabbed the phone and called Odessa.

"The first thing he did was ask how my investigation of Bud's death was going. I gave him a brief update and said I met with one of his students who was in dire need of some special consideration and a break. Then, without sharing David's name, I told him what David told me that afternoon.

"I asked if there was any way he could allow this student to resubmit a few papers on which he'd cheated. I told him the student was an aspiring engineer who thought in terms of black and white, and philosophy amounted to a 'foreign language' for him. I even offered to tutor this guy, if he could find it in his heart to allow him to make up for the invalid submissions, and missed tests and papers. I ended by telling him about the student's comment about Pierre Teilhard de Chardin. 'He even used the correct French pronunciation,' I said, 'so he had to be paying attention and trying.'

"When Professor Odessa asked how I knew he pronounced it correctly, I explained I took four years of French in high school. I added that this student knew Chardin was multidisciplinary and lamented that despite that, he could never get on his wavelength. 'Sound like an engineer to you, professor?' I asked.

"He said he knew many students were under intense pressure, and he had little trouble believing it could drive one of them to cross the line. Since he hadn't shared his suspicions with the powers that be, he said he'd meet with this student and discuss the options. He concluded by asking when David was available.

"'David?' I asked.

"'I'd been careful not to utter his name. *Had I blown it? Was it saying he wanted to be an engineer?*

"Relieving my conscience, he said, 'No, you didn't mention his name.'

"I told him I hoped it would be in the next day or two and asked if he could somehow be available over the weekend. He thanked me, said he'd be available anytime, and asked me to set up a meeting ASAP. He ended saying, 'I don't want him doing anything I'll regret.'"

THIRTY-TWO
David and Lily

"It was a bit past 10:00 p.m. I figured both David and Lily would still be up, but what about their parents? Rationalizing my next move, based in part on what Professor Odessa said, I called. I was glad when Lily answered, and I asked how David was doing.

"She said, 'The same as he's been doing ever since he came home.'

"Out of respect for David, I didn't share my thoughts or observations, or tell her what I knew. Instead, I asked if he could come to St. Jerry's either tomorrow or Sunday.

"She said she had a car and could bring him. Then she asked, 'Why?'

"I said I needed to talk to David, and maybe he'd tell her. 'And Lily,' I said, 'if he doesn't decide to come here this weekend, I'll need your help.'

"After assuring me I could count on her, she went to get him.

"The first words out of his mouth astounded me. 'Why are you calling now?' he asked. 'You said you'd call tomorrow.' It sounded like an accusation.

"I told him I was worried about him and overstepped my bounds. I assured him I didn't identify him as the

151

student when I contacted Professor Odessa to see if there was a way to save both his GPA and get credit for his philosophy class. 'The professor wants to make it work for that student,' I said and told him Odessa understands how stressful school is for all of us. 'He doesn't want to leave you hanging out there, feeling hopeless.'

"I acknowledged it wouldn't be easy, but this was his chance to undo the mistakes and missteps. With hard work, he could complete this course with a grade better than a C-minus. I'd help if he wanted and asked if he'd try.

"David said, 'Is this how you plan to turn me in for cheating, Pete?'

"'No way!' I exclaimed. 'If that's what Professor Odessa has in mind, do you think he'd be willing to sacrifice a part of his weekend? Get real. He could do that anytime.'

"David muttered, 'You're probably right.'

"When I told him he needed to get to St. Jerry's tomorrow to meet with Professor Odessa, he said that could be a problem. He didn't have access to a car. I mentioned Lily, and he said she had other plans for the weekend.

"'She loves you, David.' I said. 'Any idiot can see that. Get her on the phone with us, and we'll set it up.'

"David sighed so loud, I could have heard him if the receiver was halfway across the room.

"I pressed, 'Don't you want to make this work, David? Don't you want to get yourself back on track and earn that degree? I thought you wanted to be an engineer.'

"He said the answer to all those things was 'yes,' but he no longer believed it was possible.

"I said, 'You're the last person I'd have pegged as a quitter,' hoping to convince him to try. Then I added what I hoped would be the clincher: 'I know you can do this, David, why not make the effort? Why throw away your dreams?'

"He admitted I was right and said he'd be at St. Jerry's the next day.

"I told him Professor Odessa deserved as much advance notice as possible and asked him to get Lily on the phone with us. He did, and with Lily's help, he arranged to arrive by 1:00.

"I got Lily's email address and said I'd confirm the time as soon as I heard from the professor.

"Professor Odessa had to be watching his email, because he responded immediately. He said he'd meet the 'anonymous student' in his office at 1:00 and looked forward to designing a workable solution.

"Pleased his wording permitted it, I forwarded that email to Lily. Then I asked that she and David stop by my room on the way, so I'd know they'd made it without a glitch.

"She responded saying 'THANKS!' in a mega font."

THIRTY-THREE
David's Meeting

"Saturday, I didn't go to lunch, in case they arrived early. Thankfully, Andrea had given me the bag of leftover snacks, and I resorted to them. Not exactly an athlete's ideal diet, huh, Katie?"

"I'm so glad you've found religion," she teased.

"We had a game at 3:00 that afternoon, and I didn't know if I'd make it. I was intent on seeing David both before and after his meeting, and I wouldn't leave before I did—just in case. Besides, after missing two practices, it was unlikely I'd be allowed to play.

"David and Lily arrived at 12:30. I guess David wasn't willing to risk being late for the meeting. I took that as a good sign. And this part is even better: He wore a suit and tie. He'd showered and shaved, and his hair was combed. I can't tell you how glad I was that he made the effort.

"Since there was enough time, I took them to The Commons, bought a round of Cokes, and toasted a successful meeting. Then Lily came back to my room and kept me company, while we waited for David to return from his meeting.

154

"He arrived around 1:45, wearing a smile, and I asked if he was willing to share the details.

"He said the professor was amazed when he walked into his office. He told David that the last few papers he'd submitted had him believing 'things were clicking' for him. He asked why David never came to him if he was having trouble. David said he admitted, sheepishly, that he didn't think he had the right to ask the professor for special assistance. He'd asked a couple of other students. One said he was too busy. The other tried to help, but he couldn't make it work. He still felt lost. He told the professor that was when he resorted to stealing the information from Bud, and he wished he could apologize to him.

"The professor was working on a doable arrangement for David, and they planned to get together Monday after class.

"After sharing all of that, David looked at me and said he could never thank me enough. Then he walked across the room and hugged me.

"I told him the only thanks I needed was having him complete the class and maintain his scholarship.

"Lily hugged me too and whispered in my ear, 'Thank you! I think you just saved his life,' and she kissed my cheek."

Katie raised her hand, and Pete said, "You in the center of the front row. Got a question?"

"Being a police officer is a great way to meet women, huh?"

"Apparently so." Pete chuckled. "After all, that's how I met you, remember? The first time I saw you, you were involved in a case I was working on, and I was immediately attracted to you. But protocol and the power differential required that I wait a reasonable time before asking you out.

"When I figured enough time had passed, I tried to reach you, but only reached your answering machine. Unfortunately, I never found the courage to leave a message. Then came the fateful day when our paths crossed in the St. Paul skyways, while I was working another case. And the rest is history."

"I'll never forget it." Katie smiled warmly. "For our first date you also invited your homeless friend, Doc, perhaps to protect yourself from me ... just in case. And you barbecued steaks on the grill. But honestly, what were the chances?"

"Trust me, Katie, it would have happened one way or another. I was already committed to asking you out. I just had to succeed in reaching you."

Pete asked, "Back to the story?" and Katie nodded.

"I walked them out to Lily's car and asked David to stop and see me after his meeting on Monday. Then I ran back to my room, scrambled into my uniform, and ran all the way to the field.

"As I entered the locker room, the coach said, 'Look who decided to bless us with his presence today. We were going through the starting lineup,' he added and said I was at second! I thought my ears had to be playing tricks on me, but I was wrong. I played second that day and went three for three, including a homerun and a double!

"I noticed Professor Odessa and a kid a few years younger than me in the stands. They were there for the whole game, so I made a beeline for the stands afterwards. I wanted to thank the professor.

"'Great game!' the kid said as I approached. 'Glad to see they finally have you at second. Listening to Dad, I get the impression that in addition to being a star second baseman, you can walk on water. I want to see a demonstration sometime.' Then he broke into a gut-busting laugh.

"The professor said, 'About that meeting' and gave me a thumbs up, then congratulated me on a good game.

"As I approached my locker, Randy, a teammate, said, 'Didn't Bud ever help you with your hitting?'

"I was so shocked, I didn't say a word."

THIRTY-FOUR
Updating Andrea

"**W**hen he accepted the challenge to help David, Professor Odessa clenched a spot near the top of my list of most-respected people. Several people, including my parents, grandparents, and Uncle Pete remained secure in their standings at the top. Nothing would ever change that.

"After speaking with the Odessas, I showered, then chatted with a few teammates. In the process, I realized talking to them about Bud was getting me nowhere. Although I asked what they thought of him and whether they had any disagreements or problems with him, I realized this did little, other than eat up any available time. It seemed for more than a week I'd failed to get any additional leads, and most of my suspects were working their way off the list. Don't get me wrong, Katie. I'd continued looking for information about all of them, until I knew they couldn't or wouldn't have killed Bud.

"I also concluded that my questioning was far more productive if I had any details on the reasons the other person had a problem with or disliked Bud. That had worked with both David and Murray. So I decided that going forward, I would change my approach. I had to spend more time researching people before talking to them.

"Knowing I owed it to her, the first thing I did when I got back to my room was call Andrea. By then, she had a lot invested in my efforts, and I knew she'd want to know what happened after she dropped me off. She marveled at all I'd achieved with an email, and at the outcome. She said I was 'amazing.' I corrected her, placing the credit where it belonged—with Professor Odessa.

"Andrea insisted the professor couldn't have helped David had I not reached out to him and sold him on the need for his intercession, then succeeded in talking David into meeting with him.

"I knew I'd been nothing more than a conduit, a facilitator, but I didn't push it. Even so, I enjoyed her admiration. But most of all, I felt relieved at having helped David get on track to salvage his freshman year ... and hopefully his future.

"Then Andrea said something that blew me away. She said I should forget math and the natural sciences and move over to the social sciences, namely psychology. She claimed that my accomplishments showed that I was a natural in that field and would be wasting my time as an architect 'or whatever.' That surprised me. It was contrary to all my inclinations and career plans.

"She was thrilled that I finally got to play second, and she couldn't believe the coach did that after I'd missed two practices. She asked, 'Do you think he was afraid you might walk away from the team?' Then she suggested I miss at least two consecutive practices every week!

"I told her I didn't like living on the edge, and we both laughed.

"She said she had something exciting to tell me about returning the car to Rick. He felt guilty that I had to buy a new tire and asked Andrea to apologize profusely to me. He wanted to know how much it cost. Andrea didn't know, so he wrote a check for his best guess, and she'd already mailed it.

"I told her it was a small price to pay for the use of his car and all the miles we put on it.

"She chuckled and said, 'That's exactly what I told him you'd say.'

"When I said I wouldn't cash the check, she said he already had trouble balancing his checkbook, so that would tick him off. 'Rick's into food, not numbers,' she said.

"Each time I expressed some version of feeling guilty if I cashed it, she answered with some version of how he liked being able to help. So I gave up, and decided I'd find a way to repay him.

"'Oh my gosh,' she gasped suddenly. 'I was so excited to hear about David, I almost forgot to tell you.' She found someone who knew Kennedy Lansing and where he lives. Now she knew his dorm and room number. So far, she'd gone there twice, but he wasn't there. Deciding that could go on forever, she gave a guy who lived on Kennedy's floor five dollars and promised to give him another fifteen bucks when she succeeded, with his help, in meeting Kennedy. The person she paid became suspicious, so she had to come up with a quick explanation. She told him a friend thought she and Kennedy would be great together. The guy wanted to know why that friend didn't introduce them.

"At a loss for a good explanation, Andrea claimed it was against that friend's religion. The guy looked at her like she was crazy, so she told him to give back the money and she'd find someone else. He shrugged and kept the money. She was optimistic.

"Then she verified that the 'critical time' when he had to be in town was still between 3:00 and 4:00 on Wednesday, the last day of March. Also, if Kennedy claimed he was in class, that wouldn't cut it. She needed a time and date stamped receipt or someone trustworthy to corroborate his claim.

"After verifying all of that, I asked her to call when she succeeded ... or failed.

"She said she would succeed and told me she hoped to see me soon. Said it was a 'crazy trip,' but she had fun! I told her that went both ways.

"After hanging up, I thought about her comment about the social sciences being a better field for me. Whereas I didn't agree with her, it occurred to me that my assessments and the way I needed to stick with the investigation might point in that direction."

THIRTY-FIVE
More Time for Teddy

"**M**y professors had been understanding, but I didn't want to push my luck. So after talking to Andrea, I crammed for a physics test on Monday and worked on a paper for theology."

Katie winked and asked, "Perhaps you began reevaluating your class schedule for the fall semester, freeing up time for abnormal and social psychology?"

Pete smiled and said, "Not that night."

Katie laughed.

Pete asked, "Back to the tale of adventure and intrigue?"

"I thought you'd never ask."

"Okay, but first, here's a status report ..."

Teddy decided he was more important than a status report, and it was time for him to eat and play. While Katie nursed him, Pete headed downstairs to the basement gym and completed a quick workout with weights, sit-ups, and pushups.

He'd been unusually sedentary during his time off. Whereas he and Martin spent a lot of time in a car, traveling to meet with all kinds of people, it was rare to sit for a protracted period the way he did today. His daily run was pretty much the only exercise he'd gotten. When he estimated Katie was done nursing, he ran upstairs and joined them.

Katie was preparing to bathe their baby, and Pete was glad he arrived in time to help. He still marveled at their son's tiny hands and feet, arms, and legs. He wondered how all the necessary pieces fit in such a compact package.

When Teddy was dressed and ready to play, Pete and Katie took him back to the family room and amused him by holding out black-and-white toys that got his attention. While Teddy swatted at those things, they spoke to him, waved at him, and made faces.

Pete couldn't wait until Teddy started talking. That's when it struck him, it was crazy to rush things. He was perfectly content with this phase. Next he carried Teddy to the nursery.

Pete and Katie had painted the nursery "Lemon Chiffon" with white trim, not knowing if their baby was a boy or a girl. They'd installed white, vinyl roller shades and a sky-blue valence with white clouds. All the furnishings, including the crib, changing table with a chest of drawers, and the padded wooden rocking chair and ottoman, were gifts from family and friends. The colors were all light pastels, and the theme was Mother Goose. A frequently appreciated accessory was the musical mobile that hung over the crib.

While Pete rocked Teddy to sleep, singing *"Hush little baby, don't say a word ... ,"* Katie chatted over the phone with her parents. Once they returned to the dining room to continue with the story, Katie was thinking she knew Pete really well, but she'd learned a lot about him today.

Sitting across the table from him, she tried, and failed, to stifle a yawn.

"Does that mean you're as tired as I am?" Pete asked.

"Possibly, but don't stop now. I'm waiting for the punch line."

"Nice way to talk about my life story." Pete chuckled. "We're at least a few hours from the climax. How about waiting until tomorrow? If you don't want me to switch to the condensed version, I can talk faster, so we finish before lunch."

"Will you speak at a pace I can understand and include all the drama?"

"In that case, best guess, we'll finish by midafternoon. However, if I keep remembering details as I go along, there are no guarantees."

"Okay, let's wait until tomorrow, stick with the current pace, and include all the suspense and drama."

They went to bed. Katie slept with her head on Pete's shoulder and her hand on his chest, secure in his proximity and their relationship. He smelled like Irish Spring soap, and she loved that too.

Pete fell asleep wearing a smile. He knew he struck gold the day he stumbled into Katie in the St. Paul skyways, and he loved the path they were on. He felt blessed.

THIRTY-SIX
Chad Foxhome

Saturday was Katie's turn to take the lead with Teddy, but Pete asked to step in for his last two days at home. Knowing how important it was to him and glad it was, she agreed. After all, regardless of who took the lead, she maintained the special "mommy" connection she felt with their son whenever she nursed him.

This morning, while she nursed, Pete worked up a sweat on the treadmill. He wore a broad smile when he returned to her side. He liked running, and she wondered how the attraction remained after so many years of doing it day after day. Runners high?

After they played with Teddy, and after Pete changed his diaper and rocked him to sleep, they adjourned to the dining room. Pete again suggested they might be more comfortable in their recliners, but Katie shook her head. Unlike the family room, the dining room had them sitting face-to-face, and she didn't want to miss a single expression on his face or in his eyes.

As he shared this story, the expressions on his face, the look in his eyes, and the sound of his voice transported her into the story. They also showed, in the process, that he was reliving those days.

"Chapter thirty-seven," he began. "When we left off, I'd just been accepted at Notre Dame ..."

"Close but no cigar."

"I'd just discovered that the person who killed Bud was ..."

"Do I need to remind you where we left off?" Katie grinned.

"Nope." Pete shook his head. "Just checking."

Katie said, "I'm still hanging on every word. To prove it, you played second base during the game on Saturday. Then you evaluated your investigative technique, called Andrea, and studied. How appropriate you stopped there, since today is Saturday."

"You're my star pupil, and you get an A-plus. Are you planning on going to graduate school?"

"Already did, and not planning a return trip before we finish with this story." She loved these exchanges with him.

"Okay," said Pete. "As I mentioned, I decided to change my methodology and concentrate on uncovering any reasons anyone might have to hurt Bud, knowing things might have escalated into murder during their last minutes together. I started by searching for any link between Bud and the other person. I also concentrated on the people Bud spent the most time with, which meant the baseball team. I have to admit that made me feel like a traitor. However, my first loyalty was to Bud.

"Started with Chad Foxhome. He was the teammate Bud tutored in calculus. I had no idea how that happened, but I planned to find out and determine whether their friendship somehow evolved into animosity. Got some answers that evening.

"Chad lived in my dorm, and I went in search of him. He was a few inches shorter than me and a few dozen pounds heavier. He had shaggy medium-brown hair and eyebrows that shaded his hazel eyes.

"I wasn't optimistic, since it was a Saturday night. Unlike my earlier attempts, this time I succeeded.

"Chad said that after seeing what Bud could do with numbers, judging from all the calculations he performed for the team, he decided to approach him. Said he might not have otherwise, but he was desperate. He didn't understand calculus, and the textbook only made it worse. So one day right after practice, he caught up with Bud, explained his predicament, and offered to pay if Bud would tutor him.

"Bud spent a couple of hours explaining the next assignment and how to apply the formulas. The thing was, once was not enough, so this became a weekly event. While Chad never got an A, he started getting solid Bs on the assignments and the tests.

"Ever since Bud's death, his grades in that class had been on a downward slide, and he was getting frantic. He said the A students in the class wouldn't be bothered helping someone as 'lame' as him, and none of the other students could explain it in a way he could comprehend.

"If Chad killed Bud, it seemed, it had to be in a moment of rage, and it would have been mighty shortsighted. Even so, I changed the subject and asked what bugged him most about Bud.

"Chad smiled and said Bud was too damned smart. He nodded when I said I'd have been frustrated if someone that smart was tutoring me, because Bud would have had a hard time understanding why it was difficult for me.

"'Did you ever want to punch him out?' I asked.

"He shook his head and said there were two reasons for that, which he counted off on his fingers. First, Bud refused to take any money for helping him. Second, he couldn't risk losing Bud's assistance.

"I asked, 'Haven't you ever flown off the handle?'

"He shrugged and said, 'Never with someone Bud's size,' because it would have been too much like punching out his 'little brother.'

"That made perfect sense since he was six feet tall and about 190 pounds. On the other hand, physically speaking, and only in that respect, Bud was a lightweight. My best guess, based on our relative heights, Bud was five six or five seven. I doubted he weighed 130 pounds soaking wet, after a big meal, including a thirty-two-ounce Coke, and wearing ankle weights.

"Chad said he'd never taken a swing at his little brother, not even the times he made him crazy.

"I asked if Bud ever belittled him because of his problems with calculus. He said he anticipated it, but Bud never did.

"Chad was a good baseball player, but I didn't think he aspired to playing in the majors. Even so, failing on the math angle, I switched gears and asked if Bud gave him any baseball advice.

"He rolled his eyes, nodded, and said he 'wished Bud had kept his tutoring to calculus.'

"'Did he tick you off?' I asked.

"'No kidding,' he said. 'The guy knew math, but he never played baseball. Who was he to tell me my stance was screwed up and I needed to shorten my swing?' Chad agreed that for a time it hurt his batting average, and it frustrated him, but he never felt like 'getting even,' or so he said.

"Whomever killed Bud had to go to his room to type the suicide note on his computer. Chad said Bud always tutored him in his, Chad's, room. No exceptions. He said he'd never been in Bud's room.

"When he claimed not to know Bud's room number, I asked what he'd have done if he had to talk to him right away. He answered with a shrug, then he said Bud tutored him for a couple of months, but it was always per a preset schedule.

"It seemed highly unlikely but not impossible that during that entire time he never learned Bud's room number.

"No one was seen entering or exiting Bud's room the day he died, but I remained convinced that meant nothing. After all, Chad lived in my dorm, and I never saw Bud going to or leaving Chad's room.

"I couldn't discount Chad as a suspect, but I was at a loss for how to proceed. So I left it at that, with the possibility of a follow-up."

THIRTY-SEVEN
Another Saturday Night and ...

"**B**y the time I got back to my room following the meeting with Chad, I was exhausted and wondered how detectives did this all day long, day after day."

Katie broke out laughing and asked, "Have you figured it out yet?"

"You'll be the first to know." Pete winked.

"Despite the way I felt, I couldn't yet hang it up for the day. My conversation with Chad gave me an idea that might help point me in the right direction when approaching my teammates, and that energized me. So I created two spreadsheets, saved them to a floppy disk, and took the disk to the library. I pulled out copies of the school newspapers, starting with January 25th, which was the week Bud became the baseball team's statistician. That had me wishing there were fewer players on the team!

"It took a couple of hours to go through the team statistics and enter the data in the spreadsheets, tracking batting averages for hitters and earned run averages for pitchers. The second list was, of course, much shorter.

"Graphing what happened with both provided a visualization that made the assessment of the data fast and easy. I concentrated on the time preceding Bud's death, and the results were anything but consistent.

"The task that lay ahead was using that ammunition when I spoke with my teammates. I prioritized those whose performance deteriorated the most. But I also looked for anyone whose performance made a significant move in either direction after Bud's death. Next I created two rank order listings. One was of all the hitters and had those with the greatest deterioration at the top. The second did the same with the earned run averages. Since I wasn't in control of any schedule but my own, I knew the order in which I spoke with my teammates couldn't start at the top and follow through to the bottom. But I'd do the best I could. Figuring Bud was smiling down on my creativity, I looked heavenward and gave him a thumbs up.

"On the way back to my dorm, I passed a pitcher who was near but not at the top of the ERA list. Good enough, I thought, and I asked if he could spare ten or fifteen minutes. As an incentive, I said I'd buy him whatever from the vending machines. That proved to be both a good idea and a mistake. He met with me, and he wanted a Coke, chips, and a candy bar. I decided to reevaluate that tactic.

"The pitcher's name was Matthew Nicollet. Matt was about five ten with large biceps and triceps. I figured he tipped the scale at about 180 or 190. Either way, I thought he could easily lift Bud and toss him over the cliff. He had sharp blue eyes, curly black hair, and a mouth that appeared too large for his face.

"I asked him the questions I'd asked Chad, but geared to pitching rather than batting. He told me that

Bud had offered advice about his follow through and when he released the ball. It took Matt quite a while to get comfortable with the new moves, but he was starting to throw better. Although his win-loss record was no indicator, his earned run average and strikeouts improved. Said he was glad Bud had helped him, and he missed him.

"Thinking Matt might be able to save me a lot of time, I asked if the other pitchers felt the same way about Bud.

"He said it ran the gamut. Some incorporated Bud's advice and did better. Some couldn't make it work for them and did worse. Some ignored him and refused to try anything he recommended. When I asked who was in the middle group, he gave me three names. They were Tommy Babbitt, Austin Walker, and Chris Truman. I made a mental note of the names and asked if he knew how the other players felt about Bud. I said it was hard for me to know, because they knew Bud and I had been close.

"Matt asked what difference it made, since Bud was gone. So I asked if any of the hitters believed Bud ruined their batting average and listened for two of the names I included on that list. One was Randy Easton—the first guy Bud helped. The second was Carter Watkins. Matt said he knew more about what the pitchers thought than he did about the batters. I doubted that, but changed course and asked if he thought Bud killed himself.

"He said, 'That's the way it looks.'

"The fact that suicide remained the predominant conclusion continued to bother me."

THIRTY-EIGHT
An Assessment

"I didn't know much about law enforcement. In fact, most of what I knew or thought I knew could probably be traced back to the hours I spent watching *Law and Order* on TV. Jerry Orbach, who played detective Lennie Briscoe, was my favorite character on the show. Anyway, several things crossed my mind piece by piece during the hours I spent thinking about and working on this investigation. After my meeting with Matt, possibly because I'd created the rank order listings and thought I was getting close, those thoughts came rushing back.

"First, I thought about what it really meant for me to obtain a confession. It wouldn't be enough if I wanted the person who killed Bud to be punished. And I did. If I notified the sheriff about the confession and whomever refused to confess a second time, it was my word against his. Not good!

"That was one way the police had a huge advantage over me. Not only could they drag someone with whom they wanted to speak to headquarters, they could also record whatever that person said.

"I thought about trying to record my conversations with the people on my lists. But it would be both expensive and difficult if not impossible to carry out. I was more likely to eliminate the chances they'd talk to me than come up with a usable recording. Besides, law enforcement might refuse to grant any credence to those recordings.

"Second, if and when someone confessed, they might feel remorse ... for confessing. They might decide the next best step was to end the likelihood they'd have to pay for that confession. In other words, they'd eliminate me!

"I'd never been fearful. But until now, I'd never been this big a threat to anyone, and lots of the people who might feel threatened, thanks to me, were significantly bigger than me. I was six four and 170 pounds, but that made me a lightweight compared to lots of teammates who tipped the scale at 200 pounds and more. Since they were athletes, most of those pounds were pure muscle. Whereas I never had a desire to own a gun, and still didn't, what would I do if one of those guys attacked me?

"I decided to compensate with brains for what I lacked in brawn. Looking around my room, there weren't many useful items. I could throw a shoe. If I hit them in the face, that would accomplish little, with the exception of buying a little time. I could throw my computer or monitor and, thanks to an adrenaline rush, I could probably put some force behind it, but suppose I missed or whomever stepped aside or swatted it away?

"I had my baseball bats and could swing one at an attacker, but the police would confiscate it, and I might never get it back. I valued my equipment and wouldn't voluntarily sacrifice any of it.

"I could get a ride to town and buy an aluminum bat, but there was no guarantee the person would attack me in my room. Would I have to start carrying it around with me? If so, I had to come up with a believable excuse.

"To solve that problem, I thought about faking a limp and carrying a crutch. But most of my current suspects were my teammates. I couldn't set it aside, play baseball, and return to using it.

"I knew Bud would protect me if he could. Could he? How? I had to be more cautious, more aware of my surroundings."

THIRTY-NINE
Sunday

"**M**ass topped my list of priorities when I got up Sunday morning. I knew some divine intervention could go a long way in finding the people on my lists, getting honest answers from them, and protecting me. While praying for those I love, I decided to call three of them that day. Grandma Jackie was one of them. Thinking about her, I realized I hadn't checked my mailbox in almost a week. Had she sent a care package?

"After grabbing something to eat, the mail center was my next stop. Yes, there was a package from Grandma!

"Carrying it to my room, I contemplated the possible contents and hoped for chocolate chip cookies. The ones Lily Bellingham gave me were really good, and the fact they were still warm added to the flavor. Even so, they couldn't compare with Grandma Jackie's cookies.

"Well, there they were. The box contained chocolate chip cookies, brownies, fudge, and a bag of Chex mix. I immediately ate a cookie, smiling the whole time.

"Knowing their schedules, I didn't want to call anyone before noon. So I spent the rest of the morning hitting the books, still trying to make up for all the time I'd diverted from studying.

"At noon, knowing she always ate Sunday brunch at 11:00, and because I had a game that afternoon, I called Grandma Jackie. When she answered, without identifying myself, I thanked her for the care package.

"She, of course, knew it was me and responded saying, 'The reports of your death were highly exaggerated.' Then she laughed.

"'Yup, me and Mark Twain.'

"Since she knew about Bud, I told her what I'd been doing, including the David incident, and I described the graphs I made. I also told her about baseball and my three for three day.

"She was proud of me for helping David, and again I credited Professor Odessa.

"Grandma was glad I was at St. Jerry's. I knew it was partly because murders were unheard of there. Even so, she asked me to be extra careful. When I told her not to worry, I hired a bodyguard, she said it was 'a good start.' After congratulating me on my achievements in baseball, she updated me on the happenings in her life. She'd just joined the Retired Senior Volunteer Program, RSVP, and was enjoying it. She and her friends went to the senior center where they prepared and served meals to the elderly. She loved 'going to feed the old people,' most of whom were her age and younger, but probably less agile and many not as sharp.

"I thanked her again for the care package and told her I'd do a better job of staying in touch.

"Next I called Mom and Dad. I was glad Dad answered, because I wanted to discuss a few things with him that I didn't want Mom to hear. I told him about realizing I might get a confession but not be able to go any further with it. I said I wanted the person who killed Bud to pay.

"Dad said he knew I was right, and it was a real conundrum. He hoped the culprit would, in an attack of guilt, repeat the confession to the police.

"When I mentioned my concerns over the possibility of retaliation, Dad said he'd been concerned about that and told me to be careful. I promised I would. Then I asked him to get Mom on the line, because I had some things I wanted to share with both of them.

"After Mom picked up another phone, I told them about the rank order listing I created and how I did it. They were impressed with my ingenuity. I smiled as I told them about finally playing second base yesterday, and that I went three for three.

"Both were astounded by my ability to concentrate on the game with all I had on my mind these days. Mom said, 'You never cease to amaze me.'

"They spent another fifteen or twenty minutes telling me about all the things that were happening around home. That left me missing both them and home. I was anxious to get back to St. Paul. Christmas seemed like an eternity ago, and I'd had to stay at school for spring break due to baseball.

"As soon as we disconnected, I changed and hustled over to the stadium. The game that day wasn't a home game. We were playing at Central Lakes College in Brainerd. Randy was high on my list of priorities, and I thought about sitting next to him on the team bus on the return trip. Then I realized the bus wouldn't provide the necessary privacy. So after the game, I told him I needed his help and asked if I could buy him a hamburger when we got back to St. Jerry's. Can't begin to tell you how relieved I felt when he said, 'Heck yes!'

"The way to the truth is through a man's stomach? I wondered. I hoped so."

FORTY

Randy Easton

"**B**efore I continue," Pete said, "I need to go off on a brief tangent. I played second base again on Sunday. Only went one for three, but it was a triple deep to left field. The double play turn that Dad taught me worked like a charm—twice."

Pete pumped his fist, and Katie gave him a smiling thumbs up.

"Randy was, as I mentioned earlier, the team's power hitter, and I didn't want him knocking me into my next life. So I thought The Commons would provide a safe meeting place. We could sit in an isolated spot where others would hopefully notice and intercede if he began beating me to a pulp.

"We walked over, and I spotted a table in the back that suited my purposes as well as any. Although I knew it might provide a bit too much privacy, it was the best I could do. I bought the hamburgers and fries. Randy got two of each and a slice of apple pie. Then without argument, he followed me to the still vacant table I'd selected.

"Before continuing, to give you a frame of reference, I should describe him. Per the team data, which I'd

180

checked prior to that game, Randy was six two and
weighed 220. He had huge shoulders, muscular arms,
and massive wrists. His auburn hair was straight as a
stick. His sky-blue eyes were set far apart. He had a big
nose and a warm smile. The smile was absent when he
said, 'My turn, huh?'

"I shrugged. I wasn't shocked to learn that my
teammates discussed these meetings, but I wished I
knew how they portrayed them.

"I started by talking about how he was the first team
member Bud helped. Randy spent much of the time
nodding. Then I asked if he was glad Bud had done so.

"He said, 'Initially, no, but ultimately, yes.'

"'Were you ever in Bud's room?' I asked, and he
shook his head. He had a mouthful of hamburger, so I
was glad he answered that way ... wordlessly, I mean.

"'So you never saw the crazy way Bud decorated his
room?' I asked, and he shook his head.

"There was nothing crazy about the way Bud
decorated his side of the room, but I was watching for
Randy's reaction. If he'd seen the room, I thought he'd
know that, and a puzzled look might give him away. It
didn't work. His expression didn't change. But that
didn't deter me. I stayed the course. I asked, 'Did you
ever walk the trails with him?'

"Randy claimed, 'Until he died, I had no idea he
walked those trails.'

"When I asked if he ever walked the trails, he said,
'Rarely.'

"Sticking with that topic, I asked if the proximity of
the trails to the cliffs bothered him, and he told me no
one walking the trails could accidentally go over the
edge. He was confident Bud's fall was 'no accident.'

"Hoping to keep him off balance by jumping around between topics, I returned to baseball and asked, 'How about later, like in March, did Bud help you with your batting then?' This referred to the last month of Bud's life.

"He said he always appreciated Bud's advice, even when it resulted in a temporary slump. In the end, his hitting and ability to face new pitchers improved.

"'But did Bud help you in March?' I reiterated.

"'Got me.' He shrugged.

"Having reviewed my graphs and memorized the ups and downs in his batting average, I pointed out that he was in a slump the last two weeks of March. I didn't mention those were also the last two weeks of Bud's life.

"That was four weeks ago. If he was surprised I knew or remembered that, he didn't show it. The time frame could have been the reason he just sat there, staring at the table. He might have been trying to remember.

"I could put a time frame on my own slumps and my best weeks, but I gave Randy the benefit of the doubt, in case he didn't function that way. Carefully watching for any reaction, I said that was the two weeks before Bud died.

"He nodded and smiled, perhaps remembering, then shook his head and said, 'Sure do miss that guy, and yes, he was in the middle of helping me at the time. It was like he'd jumped ship on me.'

"'Your batting average skyrocketed a few days after he died. Were you trying to prove something to him?'

"'Randy smiled and said, 'Yeah, I was bent on proving he was right. I had to move a bit closer to and a step forward at the plate.'

"So I asked if he believed Bud killed himself.

"He sighed, frowned, and nodded.

"'Why would he do that?' I asked.

"'Obviously, he had problems,' Randy said and added, 'I don't know what the problems were. It sounds like he didn't talk about them, other than the problem with his grandpa's death, but he left a suicide note.'

"'Did he tell you about his grandpa's death?' I asked, and he shook his head. He didn't remember, or at least admit, who told him about it. When I asked if it was a teammate, he gave me a hands-up shrug.

"Not ready to throw in the towel, I asked if it was a teammate Bud had helped. The response stayed the same.

"The answer was important to me. I thought the person who killed Bud might have spread that rumor, possibly before *and* after his death, to keep the police from looking for a murderer. While I questioned Randy's veracity, at least regarding this point, I was at a loss when it came to a way to get him to talk. So I returned to the suicide note and said, 'Someone else could have typed that note.'

"All he said was, 'Mighty risky.'

"'But it's possible, isn't it?' I asked. 'How would you do it, Randy?'

"He stared at me, rubbing the back of his neck and frowning. Then he said, 'You'd have to worry about leaving your fingerprints on the keyboard, so you'd have to type using something like a pencil eraser. But that might be the easy part. If you were caught, you'd have to have a good excuse for being in his room. And you had to do it after killing him, because what if your efforts to kill him failed, and he found the note on his computer? The police would tear the campus apart, looking for whoever put that note on his computer. So why bother with a stupid note? I wouldn't have.'

"While he spoke, I began thinking he was either very thorough or thought quickly on his feet, and my suspicion that he could be the murderer grew. But the last sentence threw me. I wondered if that was his game plan."

FORTY-ONE
Andrea Reports In

"**A**fter leaving Randy in The Commons, I spent a few hours wandering around campus, looking for the people heading my lists. I didn't cross paths with a single one. That had me wondering if they were avoiding me when we weren't at practices or games.

"I did see a guy who lived in my dorm and on my floor. He had a car, so I asked if he'd be willing to give me a ride to the hardware store. There wasn't a sporting goods store in town.

"He asked what I needed. When I told him a bat, he was surprised that I needed another this late in the year. I said I'd heard about a special kind of bat and was anxious to try it. I was becoming quite the liar.

"He doubted a hardware store would have any 'special' bats, but agreed to take me to look. I knew he was right, of course, but I just wanted a bat, any bat.

"When I bought a cheap, aluminum bat, he looked at me like I'd lost it. That didn't matter. I had my new line of defense ... just in case.

"After returning from town, I carried the new bat to my room and looked for the best place to keep it. Selected a spot next to my headboard, confident that

185

would make it as accessible as anywhere. Then, having spent a decent chunk of time on Saturday dealing with two struggling students, I decided I'd better ensure I didn't join them. Finals began the week after next, and I had lots to do beforehand.

"For the next several hours, I was buried in the books, trying to catch up. I stopped only long enough to run over to The Commons for a club sandwich and a salad, working to get my diet under control. After that, I studied until Andrea called.

"She was excited and spoke so fast, I couldn't understand most of what she said. I interrupted, telling her to take a deep breath, slow down, and start at the beginning. Complying somewhat, she said the guy earned the other fifteen dollars, and right away I knew the guy she meant. He introduced her to Kennedy Lansing, and the first thing Kennedy wanted to know was what business it was of hers where he was 'on Wednesday, March 31st.'

"Anticipating that question and knowing it would be hard to produce a believable answer at the spur of the moment, Andrea was as ready as she could be. She told him she was taking part in a contest run by the youth group at her church. They gave her four names. She had no idea where they got the names, but she had to prove her resourcefulness by finding all four and proof for how they spent that afternoon, 'between 3:00 and 4:00.'

"When he asked what church, she said the Latter Day Saints. Then she had to prove they had a church in St. Cloud. Thinking it would convince him she was telling the truth, she begged him to attend the next meeting and was relieved when he said, 'No way.'

"I asked what she would have done if he said 'Yes,' and she said she was going to tell him in order to do so, he had to first be baptized into the church. I laughed and congratulated her. Who but Andrea?

"Kennedy said he spent the entire day in St. Cloud. He was in class until 3:25, then went for a beer, and he stopped and filled his gas tank on the way. He got a bit testy when she said he had to prove those things for her to be able to check his name off on her list, but asked how he could do that.

"When she said he could prove the part about the beer and the gas by showing her time-stamped receipts, he asked who kept track of their receipts.

"She started crying, so he dug through his stuff until he found them. Per Andrea, that took forever, because Kennedy was the picture of disorganization.

"He got really testy again when she asked to see the credit card, so she could match the last digits with those displayed on the receipts. But she started crying again and, grumbling, he dug it out of his billfold.

"After all that, she didn't dare ask for proof he attended the class that ended at 3:25. Just the same, per her calculations, that wasn't necessary. If Bud died between 3:15 and 4:55, Kennedy couldn't be in St. Cloud at 4:00, and that was the time on the receipt for the beer.

"I thanked her for her help and amazing ingenuity, and her ability to produce tears when needed.

"She said she had fun helping me and asked to please be included in my next investigation."

FORTY-TWO
Monday

"**M**onday started the usual way with a run, classes, then practice.

"On my way to practice, I ran into David Elmore. He looked well-rested and happy, and that made my day. Since I didn't have time to talk, we agreed to get together in a few days for a Coke.

"I wanted to know where he was staying, certain they'd never put him back in his and Bud's old room, and I was grateful I didn't have to ask. David said a student was called home because his dad was deathly ill, and he wouldn't be back that semester—a sad way to make room for him. He was in the same dorm, but up two floors. Thankfully, the reason he got that room didn't seem to rattle him.

"If I fell flat on my face with this investigation, I had the satisfaction of knowing I'd helped David. However, I didn't want to settle for that. And that was the first time it occurred to me I was running out of time. Finals began the week after next. Lots of people would be busy cramming and have good reason to put me off that week for sure, as well as much of the preceding week. What would I do if the school year ended and I had no answers? How could I deal with that?

"Practice went well. I continued playing second ... wondering how long that would last. I forced myself to enjoy it while it did.

"Three people topped the list of teammates I wanted to talk to ... or would it be more accurate to say interrogate? They were Tommy Babbitt, Austin Walker, and Chris Truman—the three pitchers Matt mentioned on Saturday. All three were in the upper quartile of my rank order listing.

"All had reasons they couldn't speak with me after practice on Monday. One said he had an appointment with a professor, another had a dentist appointment, the third was expecting a call from home that he couldn't afford to miss. I offered to meet with him in his room, letting haste take priority over safety, but he said he had to prepare for the conversation and couldn't swing it.

"I managed to meet with a hitter who was so far down on my list I hadn't planned to talk to him, unless I drew a blank everywhere else. I decided to use the opportunity to assess my methodologies and attempt to learn what the team was saying about my efforts.

"That teammate was catcher Carson Russell. While his place on the list made him a negligible risk, his size was a factor. Carson was five ten and weighed 200 pounds. He was barrel-chested and looked like he'd do fine without a chest protector when crouched behind the plate. He had big hands and a bone-busting grip, but I thought he'd spent so many hours crouched behind the plate, I could easily outrun him—if necessary.

"One benefit of meeting with a catcher is the close link between pitchers and catchers, at least on the field. I hoped he could give me another perspective on the pitchers I still wanted to corner. Lacking a better lure, and since athletes are usually hungry, I resorted to offering a meal at The Commons. Again, it worked. Had I not spent the previous weekend on the road and relied on leftover snacks for a few meals, I might have worried about the balance on my account. But I was still in good shape, and Carson went easy on me. He settled for one hamburger and one order of fries. But he topped it off with two oatmeal raisin cookies, two brownies, and an ice cream sandwich. I was anxious to see whether he was worth it.

"I began with my usual opener. Then, even though he was near the bottom of my batters list, I followed up by asking if Bud ever helped him.

"Carson asked if I meant things like the changes Bud suggested for a lot of pitchers. I nodded and asked how the pitchers reacted to Bud's advice.

"He thought the intelligent ones ignored what Bud said, though a few actually benefited.

"I said that since he was crouched behind the plate, he had an unobstructed view of how a pitcher is doing. I asked about any differences he noticed between those who benefited and those who didn't.

"Carson thought it came down to attitude, discipline, determination, and ability to take constructive criticism. So I asked if they viewed his suggestions as criticism.

"He said some did, others didn't. It all depended on the guy. He didn't take what Bud said to the pitchers as criticism, but the fact that those comments were never directed at him might have made a difference. Bud never made any suggestions about the way he crouched behind the plate, threw the ball, or batted, and he considered himself 'one of the lucky ones.'

"Trying to find a way to phrase it so Carson wouldn't clam up to protect his teammates, I asked who he thought took Bud's advice the hardest. It didn't work. He just shrugged and picked up his tray.

"I ran after him, asking whether he thought Bud committed suicide, and again his only response was a shrug. So I asked how he'd describe Bud.

"He said a smart guy whose abilities were 'misdirected' by getting so involved with baseball. I made a mental note.

"Then I asked if he liked Bud and was sorry he was gone. Carson said he thought it was 'too bad that he died at such an early age.'

"Since no other teammates were accessible, and because there were no guarantees it was a teammate, I spoke with three of Bud's other classmates that evening. Failed to uncover anything noteworthy."

FORTY-THREE

Christopher Truman

"Tuesday, I went one for three. For a hitter, that's excellent. In the major leagues, the highest lifetime batting average belongs to Ty Cobb with an average of .366 over twenty-four seasons. Second place goes to Oscar Charlston with .364, and Rogers Hornsby is third with a lifetime average of .358. So a batting average of .333 might have brought a high-buck contract offer or two. On the other hand, for a detective, it's dismal.

"That day, two of the three pitchers on my list again had, or came up with, reasons to put me off. If I had any authority, I'd have told them to make themselves available on Wednesday. But I didn't, so I couldn't.

"Christopher Truman and I met outside our dorm shortly after practice, and I asked if he wanted to go for a walk. I didn't go to my room to get the bat first, and I hoped I didn't live to regret that ... or not live and regret it.

"He stood six one and weighed 190, per the team data. Based on the wind sprints we were required to run almost every day, I thought I was quite a bit faster. If necessary, I'd depend on that.

"All of that may make it sound like I had a negative attitude or was convinced Chris did it. Neither was true. I just wanted to be prepared. Anyway, we walked to and around the quad, then began walking the perimeter of the campus. Chris started steering us in the direction of the trails where Bud died, and I balked. I told him I hadn't been able to go there since Bud's death, and he bought it. I was relieved. Even so, we were often out of anyone's sight.

"I started by asking Chris whether he'd ever been in Bud's room, and I wasn't surprised when he asked why he would have been. So I asked if Bud ever helped him with his computer. More than once, he said, but he wouldn't have carried his computer to Bud's room to get that help.

"I said I thought maybe Bud had shown him something on his computer that he, Chris, might find helpful. 'What kind of something?' he asked, and I had to scramble to create something. I made up a program that linked heart rate to the ability to memorize a list of words.

"He responded, 'It links the level of relaxation to memory, huh? Interesting.'

"In an effort to get a reaction showing whether he was lying about having been in Bud's room, I tried one other question. I asked if he saw the lunar lander Bud made out of Legos and had in his room.

"Chris said, 'For real?! I wish I'd have known about it. I'd like to have seen it. I think Legos are one of the best-ever toys, but I'm nowhere near that creative. I have to rely on the kits.'

"He convinced me ... that he was either a good actor or he hadn't been in Bud's room, since that model was in Madison, not at St. Jerry's.

"I suggested, 'No doubt Bud was a topic of conversation when you and the other pitchers were in the bullpen.'

"He laughed and said, 'A topic of conversation? That's a crazy way to ask if we talk about him. Don't you think?'

"With a straight face, I said, 'My parakeet taught me how to talk, so sometimes things come out a bit strange.' He laughed so hard, he started coughing, and I patted his back until he stopped.

"The good news was, that served as an ice breaker, and both of us relaxed. I asked if he appreciated the advice Bud gave him regarding pitching or wished Bud had kept his opinions to himself.

"Chris said, 'Both,' and it depended on the advice. He said there were times he worked for hours, trying to incorporate the advice, and often all his efforts seemed to do was throw off his timing or his concentration. While he knew Bud was generally right, he didn't aspire to playing professional ball. He just wanted to play and enjoy his time on the team.

"So I asked if that realization angered him. He chuckled and said, 'Or, speaking the way normal people do, you're asking if I ever got mad at him?'

"'Precisely, my dear man.' I said and smiled.

"Chris said that happened whenever he went for days with few strikeouts while walking all kinds of batters.

"I asked, 'Did you want to launch him into outer space at times like that?'

"He said, 'Of course,' but doing that wouldn't solve the problem. He had to decide whether to take Bud's advice or ignore it. 'It was up to me, and I couldn't blame anyone else.'

"When I asked if most of the pitchers felt that way, he started laughing and said, 'Those prima donnas?'

"I waited, hoping he'd expound on that, and he did.

"'A lot of them were the stars of their grade school, Little League, and high school teams. They came here thinking they were the next Cy Young, Roger Clemens, or Bob Gibson. Or locally speaking, if you know your Twins

194

history, Camillo Pascual, Jim Kaat, and Bert Blyleven for starters. The problem is, they need to do a reality check. *Uh oh*, I'm starting to talk like you, Pete. If I know what's good for me, I'll run for my life. What else do you need to know?'

"I said I figured these meetings were a frequent topic of discussion in the bullpen and asked what the pitchers were saying about Bud and me.

"Chris said most of the guys felt sorry for me, because I refused to accept the fact that Bud killed himself.

"'And you?' I asked.

"He said he'd gone both ways and didn't know what to think. While the reigning opinion seemed to be that Bud killed himself, he thought it possible someone had been intent on 'creating that impression.'

"I asked which team members seemed the most committed to 'selling' the suicide angle, and he said he didn't know.

"After our meeting, as he walked away from me, he turned back and said, 'You don't believe it was suicide, and you're afraid of a repeat performance, aren't you.'

"It wasn't a question, and neither his eyes nor his mouth smiled."

FORTY-FOUR

Austin Walker

"It was no surprise when Austin tried to duck out on me again on Wednesday, so I came right out and asked what he was afraid of. Most nineteen-year-old guys want the world to think they're fearless. For that reason, his hard stare bored through me as he growled, 'Definitely not you, Culnane.'

"'Prove it,' I challenged and added, 'If you weren't afraid of me, you'd find a way to give me ten lousy minutes of your time.'

"He did, and we wandered around campus with me steering us to the most populated areas. Along the way, I noticed the fresh scent of budding trees and flowers in bloom. Quickly discovered I had to shorten my stride. In addition to being about five inches taller than Austin, I have unusually long legs.

"Austin was five foot eleven, which he maximized by standing ramrod straight, and he weighed 180 pounds.

"Hoping that giving him a minute or two to cool down would improve his cooperation, I waited a bit before starting. I began by saying I liked his name and said it has a lot more personality than a name like Pete. As you know, Katie, I'm glad my name is Pete. Then I asked how he got that name, and that worked like a charm.

"Austin said his dad grew up on a farm and wanted to be a cowboy when he grew up. He had a chestnut, quarter horse gelding and showed him at the county fair and the Minnesota State Fair, and he entered several events in the rodeos.

"When his father was fourteen, Waylon Jennings recorded 'Mamas Don't Let Your Babies Grow Up to Be Cowboys.' His grandma was one of Waylon's biggest fans. She loved the lyrics and took the advice to heart. For that reason, she made his dad stop taking part in rodeos and doing anything else she believed encouraged his cowboy-related or outlaw-related dreams.

"She ran the family, and with her it was 'my way or the highway,' according to Austin. Hard as he tried, his dad couldn't change her mind, and he was too young to make it on his own. Had he been a few years older, Austin believed he'd have told her to take a hike and taken off. She changed his career path, but not his love for Texas, hence Austin's name.

"I asked what his dad did for a living, and Austin said he was an attorney. Based on the car Austin drove, I figured his dad had a hefty income. At the time, I remember wishing his dad had stayed the course and become a cowboy instead of an attorney. If Austin killed Bud and I got a confession, what were the chances he'd be convicted? I didn't let that stop me.

"Noticing our steps had taken us toward an isolated part of the campus, I wondered if this was coincidental or Austin was orchestrating it. Either way, I worked at moving us back toward a more populated region, while sticking with innocuous questions, remembering brain versus brawn.

'"Where did your dad's family farm?' I asked, trying to keep things friendly and show I was interested in him.

'"Near Royalton, and they still do.'

'"What kind of farming?'

'"Primarily dairy, grow their own hay and a few crops like corn and soybeans. It's quite the spread. One of my uncles farms with them. With his help, they recently spent a million bucks on a new milking barn or whatever they call it. Blew me away,' he said proudly and smiled.

'"Holy cow!' I exclaimed. He was not one of the players I ever hung with, so I knew little about him. That provided all kinds of additional questions. So I asked if Bud ever helped him with his computer. He just nodded.

'"In his room or yours?'

'"Mine.'

'"Did you ever see all the cool stuff he had in his room?'

'"No. Never saw his room.'

"More comfortable with our surroundings and already knowing the answer, I asked if Bud had helped him with his pitching.

'"Helped?!' he hollered, then yelled it even louder.

"I didn't say a word. Wanted to give him a chance to elaborate. It took several minutes. Absorbed in my line of questioning and his answers, I didn't realize Austin had steered us to a more secluded spot. 'In case you didn't know,' he said finally, 'I was headed for the majors. All kinds of scouts came to every game I pitched. There were never any, or maybe one, for any of the other pitchers. Just me.' He thumped his chest with an index finger.

"He continued his rant, 'I had great stuff, and several teams, including the Twins and the Yankees, knew it. They were checking me out like crazy. I might have to spend a season in the minor leagues, but I knew I'd sign a multi-year, big buck contract. I knew within a year I'd move to the majors, and within another I'd be a star pitcher. Bud screwed me royally! He destroyed my timing. He destroyed my control. He destroyed my concentration,' Austin muttered through clenched teeth. 'He changed my delivery and my windup. He claimed I telegraphed what pitch I was throwing through my location on the rubber, the way I transferred my weight, and all the stuff I already mentioned. If that was true, why did I win so many games? Even so, I did as he said. I trusted him.'

'"Then, hard as I tried,' Austin said, 'I couldn't make anything he told me I had to do work. And I couldn't go back to what came naturally—what always worked for me. When I tried, those things no longer worked. He ruined me!' By now Austin's face was scarlet and he was throwing his arms around and swinging wildly.

'"But Austin,' I interrupted, 'your ERA improved before Bud died and ...'

"He cut me off, shouting, 'Yeah, like that matters! Did you pay any attention to the teams and batters I was up against? They were the worst. The teams had laughable win-loss records, and most of the batters had batting averages under 200. My ERA meant nothing! Every pitcher has a bad day here and there or even an occasional streak of bad days, but after Bud totally screwed up my pitching, I had a never-ending *series* of bad days. I went from striking out the best batters to giving up a lot more singles, doubles, and walks. The scouts knew that, and that's why they abandoned me. The games I pitched no longer meant anything.'

"He took a breath and continued, 'First the number of scouts started shrinking. Now most days you'll find zero or one ... even if you launch a search party. Bud's advice destroyed me and my career!' His shoulders slumped and his head hung.

"I listened wordlessly as he continued, 'I'm a senior, my major is sociology, and I have a C-plus average. I never bothered to spend much time studying, because it wasn't like I was ever going to be a sociologist. So why should I care about GPA? Now what am I going to do? Farm with my grandparents and my uncle? No way in hell!'

"I increased the distance between us, wondering if he was going to take a swing at me, if not for asking these questions, then for having introduced Bud to the team. That proved to be either a premonition or my guardian angel watching over me. He thrust out his chin and his eyes bore into mine as he said none of this would have happened were it not for me. He said he'd had three successful years at St. Jerry's, then I arrived, and it all went to hell. I poisoned the well. He asked if I'd like to join Bud. Said he'd be happy to throw me into the same ravine where he'd tossed Bud. He was sure Bud would like to see me, and maybe we could screw up baseball in heaven ... or more likely in hell. That's what both of you 'deserve,' he snarled.

"Then he lunged at me, grabbing for my shirt."

FORTY-FIVE
Moment of Reckoning

"**R**unning for all I was worth, I thanked God for adrenaline. The door for my dorm room wouldn't even slow Austin down, but at least I had a bat there. I hoped he wouldn't attack me if people were around. What time was it? Would everyone on my floor be at dinner? I thought, *Oh Lord, why wasn't I smarter? Why didn't I select a safer spot to elicit a confession?*

"I'd not only proved that Bud didn't kill himself, I'd also found the murderer. That would do his parents a world of good, but only if I was able to notify them. *What if I die today?* I thought. They knew I was out to find Bud's murderer. If I die in the process, will I only compound their misery?

"I wanted to know how close Austin was, whether he was closing in on me. Much as I wanted to look back over my shoulder, I couldn't. That would slow me down, and a single step could mean the difference between life and death.

"I listened for the sound of footsteps, breaking branches, anything that would tip me off to his proximity. If it were fall rather than spring, crunching dead leaves would tell me how close he was and whether he was gaining on me. It might even indicate it was time to try to land a few punches before he took me down.

"Before he snapped, I'd worked our way back to a less-isolated area. But I was caught up in his confession and hadn't noticed how alone we were by the time he decided I should 'join' Bud.

"*Will you be there when I cross over, Bud?* I wondered. *How about you, Uncle Pete?*

"Suddenly, much as I wanted to live, I knew dying wouldn't be all bad. I hoped I'd also get to meet my Grandpa Schmitt. *If I do, I'll say hi for you, Grandma Jackie,* I thought.

"Anxiety-induced exhaustion set in too quickly, and I wished I'd had a Coke after practice. The caffeine and sugar might have helped at a time like this. That's when I heard the first indication of Austin's location—a loud grunt. Fearing I knew what that meant, I glanced over my shoulder and saw him lunging for me.

"I reacted and did what came naturally. I jumped to the side and ducked. The class ring he wore on his ring finger caught my right cheek, and that stung, but it was nothing like a full body blow.

"With a miraculous burst of energy, I sprinted for my dorm, then I heard his cry of pain. He'd hit the ground, arms outstretched, and landed hard on his belly. That had to hurt. I hoped it took the wind out of him.

"Knowing this might be my last chance, I ran faster than ever before, grabbed the door, and dashed into my dorm. Though I couldn't hear him, he couldn't be far behind. I got inside my room, locked the door, and grabbed my new bat, aware neither provided much protection. While it was a darn sight better than nothing, I knew Austin could break down the door with one swift kick.

"Bat in hand and facing the door, I called 911. When an operator answered, I said I was in my dorm at St. Jerry's, gave her the dorm name, room number, and my name. I told her a guy was out to kill me. I said if they didn't arrive soon to 'please tell my parents and grandparents I love them.'

"Then I explained that the guy who was out to kill me was Austin Walker, a senior at St. Jerome's, and he'd just admitted he murdered Sterling Callaway on March 31st. I added that I knew the sheriff's office was investigating that death because I wanted her to send people familiar with Bud's case.

"She said she was sending help and instructed me to stay on the phone with her. I said I would, but told her if the police or sheriff didn't arrive in a few minutes, I'd probably be missing or beaten to death. I said I wasn't making it up or exaggerating.

"I couldn't check the time, unwilling to transfer my concentration from the door for even a nanosecond, while listening for the sound of someone grabbing the doorknob. I'd locked the door but, like I said, that couldn't delay Austin for more than a few seconds.

"My mind raced as the 911 operator chatted away in the background, and I answered by rote with a series of *uh-huhs* and *yeahs* that may or may not have been appropriate, based on whatever she was saying.

"*Where are you the one time I need you, Scott?* I thought, referring to my roommate. That's when I heard the sirens.

"Where was Austin? He couldn't take this long to reach my room, even if he'd had the wind knocked out of him. Did he hurt himself that bad? Was he lying there, injured? It made no sense.

"To prove he was the one, I should have asked Austin how he did it, where along the trail, and the time. If the police arrived in time, would they believe Austin did it? *What if I'd put him in attack mode and made myself his next target for nothing? ... other than the satisfaction of proving I was right and finally knowing who did it?*"

FORTY-SIX
Deputies Take Charge

"The next thing I knew, someone pounded on my door and a deep, demanding voice yelled 'Sheriff! Open up!'

"I probably wouldn't have believed him, but I knew that wasn't Austin's voice. So I placed the handset on my bed and rested the bat against it, not wanting the bat to raise their suspicions or alarm them. I cautiously opened the door—just a crack. Found myself facing four uniformed deputies. I took a breath of relief. 'I'm glad to see you!' I raced through Bud's death and Austin's confession and said I'd been sure Austin would get to my room before they did. 'He threatened to kill me!'

"With his arms crossed over his chest, the guy who demanded entry growled, 'We're here now, kid. Don't you think you should leave the investigations up to law enforcement?'

"I wanted to tell them that they'd been working the case about four times as long as me, and best I could tell they hadn't come up with anything. Thankfully, Dad and Mom taught me respect, so rather than sharing my opinion, I said, 'Yes, Sir.'

"He asked if I had any idea where Austin might be, since he obviously wasn't in my room.

"'His room?' I suggested. Then it struck me, and I said, 'Or maybe he took off in his car.'

"The deputy, whose nametag said Savage, and who seemed to be taking the lead, sent two officers to recruit assistance from campus security and conduct a campus-wide search.

"'He's a big guy and he's dangerous—desperate and out of control,' I called after those deputies.

"'What kind of car does he drive?' Savage asked.

"'A red Corvette,' I said and added, 'He parks in Lot 4.'

"While Savage, his partner, and I ran there, Savage radioed the officers searching the campus for Austin. He told them he was headed for parking lot 4 and to watch for a red Corvette. Before disconnecting, he asked me if there were any other red Corvettes on campus. I shook my head.

"Lot 4 wasn't that big, and I couldn't see it when we were still almost a block away. I was sure it wasn't there. I told Savage that, and he said we'd check to make sure we didn't miss it. *How do you overlook a red Corvette?* I'd wondered.

"After we struck out, he asked if I had any idea where Austin might go in his car. Again, I shook my head.

"Then he asked where Austin's parents live, and I said I didn't know, but some of the other baseball players probably did. As we walked back toward their car parked near my dorm, I stopped dead in my tracks, remembering, 'His grandparents have a dairy farm near Royalton! He could hide the Corvette in a shed or the barn or ...'

"'Royalton?' Savage said. 'That's about forty-five minutes south of here.' He looked me in the eye and said, 'You'll recognize Austin Walker. Want to ride along? If you do, you have to follow *all* my instructions to the letter.' I nodded wildly.

"Savage, his partner Wilder, and I ran to his patrol car. As soon as we'd buckled in, he hit the road while his partner updated the other officers on the campus, then put out a statewide BOLO (be on the lookout) for a red Corvette. Lastly, he called the Morrison County Sheriff's Office and asked if there was a dairy farmer with the last name Walker in the Royalton area.

"The dispatcher knew the family and provided directions. Then he asked her to send a patrol car to meet us at the Walker farm. Hearing all that, I hoped that was where Austin went. I had this feeling he had, but that didn't mean anything.

"Thanks to the directions provided by the dispatcher, we went straight to the Walker farm. As we pulled up to the farmhouse, a Morrison County deputy walked over to the driver's door. Savage got out and shook his hand. I heard little of what was said, but they left me in the car while they and Wilder went into the farmhouse.

"About ten minutes later, Savage and Wilder returned to the car, with Austin Walker in handcuffs.

"Wilder sat in the back seat with Austin, and I rode up front with Savage."

Katie asked, "How did it feel being that close to the guy who killed your buddy? How awful!"

"Yes, it was. No one said a word the entire time. They took Austin to the sheriff's office, then Savage found someone to drive me back to campus.

"Before I returned to St. Jerry's, Savage thanked me for the help in locating Walker.

"I asked if he'd let me know if Austin confessed.

"'In good time,' he said.

"Having no idea how to measure 'good time,' I said, 'Sir, if you release Austin on bond or outright, I won't be safe. And that won't change even if the semester already ended. There aren't that many Culnanes. He'll find me. Did you see the way he looked at me when you brought him out to the car? Pure hatred. I'm not a cop. I don't own a gun.'

"I continued, 'He drives a Corvette. He has access to all kinds of resources. I can't afford a car at all. What do you think my chances are up against someone like Austin? I also fear for my family. You were right. I should have left it up to law enforcement. If I show up dead, rest assured he had a hand in it.' I'd realized all those things while sitting in the patrol car at the farm.

"By the time I'd finished, my forehead was dripping wet, and I could feel sweat trickling down my back.

"Savage stood a moment staring at me. Then he smiled and said, 'I'm confident you needn't worry, son. When we arrived, he blew up and confessed what he'd done. He wasn't smart enough to keep his mouth shut. Not even Miranda stopped him, and three deputies witnessed and heard it all.'"

FORTY-SEVEN
Sharing the News

"**A**fter thanking the deputy for the ride, I raced to my room. Scott wasn't there, and that was a relief. I had a lot of calls to make, and this way I wouldn't have to speak guardedly.

"First, I called the Callaways. Win answered, and I asked if he could get his mom and dad on the phone with us.

"It took a minute or so, but when I had all three of them on the line, I told them about my meeting with Austin and Deputy Savage.

"In response, all I heard was happy screams. After she calmed down and collected herself, Bud's mom told me I was her hero. His dad said Bud and their whole family were so lucky Bud and I became friends. He'd never be able to thank me adequately, and if there was ever anything he or the family could do for me, all I had to do was mention it. Win said he hoped he and I could be as good of friends as I'd been with Bud, and he wanted to give me a car.

"Concerned about leading them to the wrong conclusions, I said there was no guarantee of a conviction. None of them cared.

209

"'All that matters,' Mrs. Callaway said, 'is we know Bud didn't kill himself. We never really believed it, but it was always there, hanging over our heads. Thanks to you, we can place it behind us ... and we will.'

"They knew about finals, but wanted to know if there was any way we could get together—soon, and Win said he'd come and get me.

"I promised to figure out my schedules for finals and baseball, and let them know.

"Win stayed on the line after his parents hung up. I told him Austin blamed Bud for his problems, but Bud was right about Austin and his pitching. I explained that as a batter, I spent lots of time studying pitchers, looking for patterns. Also told him about the *Sports Illustrated* book called *Baseball,* and how in that book, both Harmon Killebrew, in his chapter on hitting, and Al Downing, in his chapter on pitching, talk about the very things Bud zeroed in on. Per those all-star pros, Austin did great while up against college players who would never make the major leagues. Had he gotten to the majors, the players at that level would have quickly gotten his number, and his ERA would have suffered.

"In the major and minor leagues, I said, I believed pitching coaches would have demanded the changes Bud recommended. Had he failed to succeed in applying them, I thought at best he'd have spent his whole career with a farm team, not as the major league star he imagined himself to be.

"Win told me I was awesome, and he couldn't even begin to thank me enough. Said between my visit, which gave his parents hope, and today, he wished he had a way to express his appreciation adequately. He ended by saying, 'I know Bud is giving you a thumbs up. I love you, pal.'

"It took a minute for me to compose myself, then I made the second call."

"**D**ad and Mom were next on my list. I knew Dad would want to know about my day, and I needed to share my success with him and Mom.

"Mom answered, and I asked her to stay on the line and get Dad.

"She said, 'If you didn't sound so happy, I'd be scared.'

"'What's the good word?' Dad asked.

"I told them about my meeting with Austin, minus any details that might make them nervous or fear for me. Dad said he'd been waiting for this news, and Mom said the police needed more people like me.

"That hit me right between the eyes."

"**V**alerie had a right to know, and I didn't think I should tell her over the phone. So I checked the schedule for The Link, then called. When she answered, I said I wanted to see her and would be there in forty minutes. She promised to meet me at the entrance to her dorm.

"She was there, as promised. I took her hands in mine and shared the news. She was happy to know for certain Bud hadn't killed himself, appreciated my tenacity, and cried. I held her until she was cried out, then told her I knew Bud loved her. She nodded, gave me a weak smile, and returned to her room.

"I was glad I did it the way I did."

"Of course I had to tell Andrea, so I wrapped up the day doing that.

"She was thrilled and relieved. The end!"

FORTY-EIGHT
The Bottom Line

Pete pushed his chair back from the table, stretched, then walked around to Katie, pulled her to her feet, and gave her a long hug and kiss. He reveled in her light, flowery smell.

"*Whew,*" he said, "I feel like I just conquered Everest."

"You became a police officer, so you could have the authority to make a real difference?" Katie asked. "That way, the next time you tried to fix an injustice, you would have the tools? . . Or was it because Win gave you a car?" Katie teased.

"As you well know, Katie, blue is my favorite color. So I joined the St. Paul Police Department instead of becoming a Ramsey County deputy sheriff. Their uniforms are black and gray. And how did you know Win followed through and gave me a car? In fact, he gave me that 1973 Monte Carlo he was restoring and was so proud of. It was dark brown with a chamois vinyl top. I fell in love with that car and drove it for twelve years." Pete smiled as he reminisced.

"But when it comes to the real reasons, here are the facts, which I'm sure you already know. I felt grateful to

213

have found the man who murdered Bud for several reasons. Probably the most important was how much it meant to his family, and that made me feel as happy as I had ever been ... to that point."

He reached down, grasped her hand, and kissed her again, remembering those good feelings.

"Then came getting justice for Bud and ending the still commonly held belief that he'd killed himself. Whereas suicide no longer meant the Catholic Church couldn't or wouldn't bury you, it had a stigma attached, and it still does. I didn't want Bud's name to carry that burden. Finally, there was the satisfaction of knowing I'd done it. I was instrumental in obtaining justice for everyone affected by Bud's murder. Being able to help David in the process was a bonus too."

"The way you care about people is just one of the reasons I love you so much," Katie said and wrapped her arms around him.

Pete hugged her tightly, feeling and remembering the poignancy of those days when he had the chance to help make such a difference to Bud's family.

Teddy had been patiently entertaining himself in his crib, but decided enough of the storytelling. It was time to eat.

While Katie got situated, Pete left to get Teddy. Wearing a smile, he handed their son over to his mom. He loved the happy and contented look on Katie's face while she nursed Teddy. With a surge of love for his family, he said a quick prayer of gratitude for his many blessings.

Pete and Katie turned in early that night. He was trying to catch up on sleep, before returning to work, and she was preparing to go it alone.

FORTY-NINE
Mixed Emotions

An hour earlier than would have been necessary before Teddy's arrival, Pete completed his daily run on the treadmill in the basement. He had an audience of one—their dog Benji.

As soon as Katie and Teddy woke up, he joined them. He didn't want to forego any opportunity to help. His ability to do so was about to be reined in drastically.

At 6:30 a.m., with mixed emotions, he kissed Katie and Teddy good-bye at the back door and left to resume his duties as Commander Culnane, a detective with the St. Paul Police Department. He didn't yet know how long that would last.

ACKNOWLEDGMENTS

My thanks to Mark Kempe, retired investigator, St. Paul Police Department; and Don Gorrie, retired chief investigator, Ramsey County Medical Examiner's Office. Any errors in those areas are the result of my misinterpretation or misapplication of the information these people so generously shared.

Thanks to Pat Harper, Christopher Smith, Pam McCord, Valerie Olson, Kris Olson, Jen Smith, Ethan Smith, Ellie Smith, Jackie Harper, and Dale Smith for their research assistance.

I'm also grateful to Ruth Krueger, Rick Winter, Arlene Carpenter, Deb Harper, and Marly Cornell for sharing their proofreading and editorial expertise; and Christopher Smith for sharing his time and computer expertise.

Other books by S.L. Smith

Blinded by the Sight
Running Scared
Murder on a Stick
Mistletoe and Murder
Murder on Cathedral Hill
Last Breath
Dead Reckoning
A Party to Murder

Made in the USA
Middletown, DE
12 September 2024

60223469R00124